Visions of the Future, Volume 11

Ephemeris

by
Julian M. Miles

Printed via Amazon KDP.
Available from Amazon stores worldwide, and other retail outlets.

The eBook is available for Kindle from Amazon stores worldwide, for Apple devices from iTunes, and for all other devices from Smashwords.

British Library Cataloguing in Publication Data. A catalogue record for this book is available from the British Library.

Design and layout by Julian M. Miles
Original cover art by Simon J Mitchener
Photograph of Julian M. Miles by Maricel Dragan. All rights reserved.
365 tomorrows logo used with permission. All rights reserved.

Visit us online
Lizards of the Host Publishing: www.lothp.co.uk
Julian M. Miles (a.k.a. Jae): www.lizardsofthehost.co.uk
Simon J. Mitchener: www.simonjm.deviantart.com
365 Tomorrows: 365tomorrows.com

To Gary P.
You always said I should.
So I did.

Contents

Enthusiasts 1

Chains 4

Epic Humanity Failure 7

Salvage 10

Eternal Fire 13

Proximity Causes 17

Scores 20

Warnings 23

Sad Songs 26

Red Boat, Blue Boat 29

Via Tenebrae 34

New Friends 37

Romeo and Julius 40

Witch Hunts 43

Wolf Now 46

The Specimen 48

Mischief 51

I Give the Guns 54

On a Sunny Afternoon in Kentucky 57

Clearance 60

Monsters of All Sizes 62

Revelation 65

Harrowed 68

Girls' Night Out 71

Broken Wings 75

Vindictive 78

Finding the Truth 81

Requiescat 84

Observers 87

Dirty Badge 92

Why Did You Run? 95

The Peace of Fireflies 98

"It is a Land of Poverty..."..101

Ghostsong..104

Page 314 107

New Record...109

Mind Your Step...112

VacSinHate...115

Go, Now..118

Patient Y..122

Bite Back 125

"Run Where, Do What?"..127

Fort Anger...130

Proof Positive...133

Stare Down...136

The Eternity Suit..138

Time Scars...141

Mystery Man..144

War More 147

VaccinState 151

Pellucid...154

Home Again...157

Lochstein's Gambit...160

How Many Times?..163

Take a Breath..168

Forge..171

Family Tree..173

The Men in the Moon..176

Letting Go...183

I Am Leg End...186

Circuits in the Sky...189

My Name is Drastic...193

The Forest Ring..196

Enthusiasts

Two guns: one an Earther automatic, the other a Lenkormian beamer.

"Holy Marduk, that's a Grifone!"

And we have an enthusiast. I grin at the young trooper.

"Only by looks. It's a custom Perez .557 automatic. I spent some time at his compound when I was stationed in Lima."

He points to the white-steel death on my other hip.

"Lenk or Kor?"

I do like a being who knows their xenohistory.

"Lenk body, Kor chassis. Genuine Lenkormian cell."

He goes whiter than the weapon we're discussing.

"A Forever Gun?"

I nod. Any second now...

He starts to bring his rifle up. The Forever Gun flits from its holster to be in my hand by the time I need to think 'fire'. The beam goes through his right eye and exits through the left parietal.

There's a shout from behind: "Stand down! Your fancy beamers won't cut cerasteel."

I turn to face the armoured warrior with lieutenant's stripes on the left chest. A man with that many service bars should be better than enthusiasts like the one I just killed. I level the Perez at him and put an armour-piercing round containing depleted uranium pellets floating in liquid Teflon through his stripes. Either load would be sufficient, but the excessive blend seems to really upset the people we need to annoy.

He hits the floor, blood already seeping around the torso plates. I hope they open him in a container. It'll take ages to clean the smaller bits off a floor.

"I recognise that cannon blast. Have you started, Red?"

My overwatch. As the cliché goes: if you think I'm nasty, just hope I don't need her to intervene.

"Ran into a gun collector at the gate. He recognised the combo."

"Didn't the cannonball go straight through?"

"That was mincing his Lieutenant."

"Didn't think you'd waste a shot. Okay: target is in the central compound."

"That's three gates and a couple of towers away?"

"Yes. While I would never doubt your abilities, it might be an idea to flush game."

I'm dangerous, but without my war machine about me, the second fire tower will turn me into prime cuts and carbon. Jogging towards the next gate, I use the Forever Gun's ridiculous range to drop all three troopers before I get there. Sadly, I have to shoot their Lieutenant in the back as he's too busy running. Never put a soft officer on critical duty.

"General Ranno! Remember the Twenty-First Keshichan Lancers? I'm Khevtuul Chloe Bastia, and I'm here to end your days!"

Four years ago he led us into an ambush. He used that betrayal to get himself a promotion into the enemy ranks, going from Cherbi to General at the cost of the people who trusted him.

"Nicely over-the-top, Red. He's moving."

"Away from me?"

"You need confirmation?"

"As a Khevtuul, I reported directly to him. If he's not running, that's a body double. Politics and cowardice were his only competencies."

"He's exited the central compound, heading away, but slowly."

"Do I need to crack another gate?"

"Use something splashy."

I point the Perez at the distant gatehouse and thumb the integral laser designator. In the car park across the road, an assault drone ruins its camper van disguise by sending something fast with a thermobaric warhead to do my destroying.

As flaming bits of gate and soldiers rain down, I hear a chuckle.

"*Konnichi wa*, General-*kun*."

The sky lights up as Saeko-*chan* fires the anti-ship beamer she affectionately calls 'Torchy'.

"He's done. Spread like smoking geography. Let's go home."

"Thanks."

"Anytime. I love killing things with you."

That's my girl.

Chains

The viewing room is hushed as we approach the co-ordinates. Every being not on duty has gathered. For some, it's a rite of passage. For others, a renewal of faith.

"Exiting shiftspace in three, two, one."

Conventional space and time welcome us back with their usual indifference. As the spinning greyness streams away like impossible mist, distant stars catch our eyes. Then it becomes clear, and everything else is irrelevant.

You've seen the descriptions of Artaxerxes. Might even have seen a blurry image or two. If you're lucky, you've seen one of the captures from the first mission. No matter how you came to be aware of it, nothing can prepare you.

At some point before life appeared on Earth, it had been a habitable planet. Now, it's a wandering mystery.

We've mapped this battered sphere, can show you depictions of what it used to be like, with deep oceans and continents much like Earth was during the first millennium of man's dominance.

Except for the chains.

Those impossible artefacts, anchored deep within opposite sides of the planet by means we're still trying to grasp, trail back for nearly twice the planet's diameter. One side has four links, the other five. The broken links of either side have been lost somewhere on the journey. They certainly aren't anywhere nearby, so their loss must have happened long ago.

Not as long ago as the event that launched this world upon its lonely travels. Something so vast we struggle to imagine. What was this planet chained to? There are many theories. My favourite is that there were many worlds arranged to form a necklace around a star for reasons we'll never work out. The one that still makes me laugh is where some gargantuan spaceship carries planets as weapons.

Our finds under the surface of Artaxerxes have only increased the mystery, resulting in the entire project placed under a veil of secrecy.

The inhabitants of this place looked like humans! The murals we've found hint at a society much like nineteenth century Europe, except for a pervasive religion that more closely resembled that of Ancient Egypt. No writings have survived, bar the minimal notations etched into rocks in caves far below the surface.

Artaxerxes was cast adrift so long ago that organic traces are gone. Judging by the condition of the surface, it has endured incredible heat at times along its journey. We're sure that some survived the initial cataclysm. Most of us agree that the etchings in the rock of the deep caves were made by the last of them. Sadly, we've found no equivalent of the Rosetta Stone from which to make a translation.

Backtracking the course of this planet indicates an origin further towards the expanding edge of our universe. Some are convinced it's not of this universe. I'm not one of them. Yet. We simply don't know. That's why I've lived here for decades, only returning to the worlds of the Accord when I have to. Somewhere in this hurtling mystery is the clue we need. One of them must have predicted this would happen: that some other race would find the remains of their home.

"Welcome back, Professor Tessen."

I nod to the security guard. This year's intake of students and recruits follow me into the converted battleship that keeps pace with Artaxerxes to serve as our base.

Maybe this is the year we'll find that clue. I don't care if it's not me. I just want someone here to earn their place in history, whilst giving me a lead at last.

Epic Humanity Failure

"Looks like it used to be a nice destination."

"It was. Had forests in more shades of green than you'd believe possible."

"The usual problems?"

"Yes and no."

"Do tell. We're here until we finish checking the place. Got to make sure there's nothing that'll hinder its regeneration or anything that could affect the next indigenes. Once that's done, it should make a decent colony world - after another couple of hundred revolutions round the star."

"If it comes back like it was, I'll petition to be allowed a home here."

"Tell me about them."

"They called themselves humans. Primate origin from saurian splice."

"Another experimental world?"

"That's why I first came here. Got assigned to investigate. Turns out this was a world jumped forward by renegades. No purpose but to give the locals a head start."

"Unusual. So, they got kicked into sentience early. How did that work out?"

"About as well as you'd expect, but with some notable exceptions. Getting intelligence before they worked through their tribal urges gave them some unique advantages, along with the usual problems."

"Hierarchal societies, either declared or concealed. Constant warfare underpinned by varying forms of fanaticism and greed. Stagnation of societies between changes forced by non-combatant adaptations to conflict. Further friction caused by attempts to return to pre-war societal structures after each of the bigger conflicts. I presume they added rampant technology to the mix?"

"They did. Quite stunningly, I have to add. Went from grounders to spacers very quickly."

"I'm guessing their societies didn't evenly reflect those advances?"

"Correct. Poverty and treadmill lower tiers overseen by a minority that eventually held wealth beyond imagining."

"I can see where this is headed. Exploitation, pollution, and planetary exhaustion. But why did they not head to the stars? You said they rapidly developed space flight."

"My investigations indicate some repressive factions amongst those with wealth determined that the cost/benefit ratio could erode the accrual rates of their wealth. So they stifled it using political manipulation."

"What we're finding below doesn't show a slow decline."

"Something changed. For all that they still carried the detracting factors of their forced evolution, they had moments of selfless glory and vision. Towards the end of their time, a great war occurred. It ruined whole sections of the planet and left the survivors facing starvation. One of those glorious moments happened. Surviving nations forgot their squabbles and started to collectively build giant spaceships. The ships were intended to take as many humans as possible out into the universe. Initially to the next furthest planet from the star, then onwards if necessary."

"Workable. We've seen it done before."

"The colony ships were marvels of ingenuity. Everything they had came together to create fully landscaped environments within five great spaceships."

"What went wrong?"

"Some of the wealthy recruited armies of the fanatical to protect the havens they'd already built on the next planet out."

"Those tiny ruins on that red planet back there?"

"The very same."

"They didn't look self-sufficient. Were they?"

"Only in their deluded belief. Similarly, for gene pool size and continued existence, they had specialists claiming that cloning and genetic manipulation would save them all."

"The colony ships, built to save the race, were sabotaged by servants of those who only wanted to save parts of the race? So, as the ships failed, unconstrained war broke out over access to the surviving ships?"

"Yes and yes."

"What about the one embedded in their moon?"

"Crashed attempting to get behind it to evade attack. There were no trained pilots amongst the mutinous faction on board."

"A sad coda."

"To a spectacularly stupid extinction."

Salvage

"Hey, Pete. What's the name of this station again?"

"Celeste."

"Appropriate."

"Hush up, Davy. Get back to duty or the captain will murder us."

"If he does that, he'll have no-one to pilot or fix the ship."

"Good argument, but I don't want to listen to another of his speeches."

"That's a better argument."

"Okay. So: what's in the box, Davy?"

"Nothing, Pete."

"Thank you for that. What was in the box?"

"No idea."

"Scan the transit data."

"There isn't any."

"Davy, the logistics computer told us about this anomalous box. Therefore, it was scanned."

"Could the box be anomalous because it's here without transit data?"

"Give you that. Okay, describe the box."

"Can't you see it?"

"No. The internal cameras are down in some sections."

"So you can't see me?"

"The captain can see your biotelemetry. I have nothing."

"It's a metal box. Two metres long, one high, one wide. There's a nine-point locking mechanism in the lid, with an external lever."

"Who'd open an unidentified shipment?"

"Don't think that was the problem. See this?"

"No, Davy, I don't. What is it?"

"There's a hole in the lid. About a hundred mil in diameter. The metal is curled outward. It's right next to where the lever is now."

"You think something punched through the lid and let itself out?"

"Yes."

"How thick is the metal?"

"About ten mil. It's a laminate. Middle layer must be what prevented scanning of the contents."

"Not unusual. But you think an unknown something arrived in a box from we don't know where, got itself loaded into the holding bay, then let itself out and is now roaming the station?"

"Makes more sense than mass hysteria causing everyone to jump into the lifepods and leave."

"So, after dumping the lifepods to hide its presence, what did it do with the bodies?"

"How many could you fit in an airlock if you stacked them?"

"On this ship? Standard four-suit locks, so I'd guess five across, maybe eight high."

"Around 40, then. How many lock cycles have there been in the last week?"

"Apart from us, three. That's odd. All Lock B, and at four-hour intervals. Last one was midnight last night."

"How many crew should there be?"

"Around a hundred."

"The math works."

"Davy, why? Why would some lethal thing be sent here? It makes no sense."

"Pete, this station is the furthest out. If you wanted to test something, this is the place."

"Test?"

"To see if the plan to get it in here works. To see how deadly it is."

"They'd have to monitor it."

"Not if it went back to report."

"In a pinnace? The range is tiny. Even if it scavenged the lifepods for boosters."

A huge vibration shakes the station.

"Pete, what was that?"

"Hang on, Davy."

"Pete?"

"Davy, that was our ship explosively undocking. Passive displays show it's pushed the station out of stable orbit."

"We can presume the captain is dead, then."

"Cold but true."

"Is this station really dead?"

"Absolutely. Even the orbit stabilisation systems are useless."

"Then I'll start tearing out communications gear and filling the second pinnace. Even if it's been smashed up inside, we should be able to launch into atmosphere and survive the landing. You grab as much food and water as you can."

"Don't forget charge packs, Davy!"

"Good reminder. How long do we have?"

"No idea. Let's get off this death sentence as soon as possible."

"See you in pinnace two."

"Looking forward to it. Well, the not dying bit, anyway."

"Love you too. Get moving."

Eternal Fire

"You will die here, warrior. Your newly inherited title will ensure that."

Erismaeus has always been honest. Now his brows knit.

"I can save you, but it will be an exile like none have ever told. There will be no return in glory."

I look up from my slump on the cave floor, lifting the hem of a torn and blood-soaked overshirt.

"Return to what exactly, wizard? My family, clan, lovers, and friends have all been slain. They even killed my backers, and anyone I owed honour or favour to. I only avoided dying by having to use the garderobe at the right time."

Erismaeus crouches down, a look of concern on his face.

"I know of a place, a land at war, yet unbedevilled by gods or magicians."

"Do it. My blessings for risking what little you have to save me. Will we meet again, magus?"

"No. Go now, Ruben. Find fortune forever."

I saw the spirals of magic as he spoke, my vision went grey, then I landed in ashes, the smoking ruins of a town about me. My first experience of this world's warfare was a crooked-winged warbird screaming by overhead, pursued by a silver eagle that spat fire from its wings.

Anything that sounds like a diving Stuka still makes me look for cover.

I wake with that noise and his words ringing in my mind: 'Find fortune forever'.

If only he'd said that before starting the working. The one question that haunts me is if he intended it to be some recompense for the losses I'd suffered?

In the century since my arrival, I've fought my way round this 'Earth' thrice. I've been buried nineteen times, had two funerals at sea, and been left for dead more times than I can remember. A legacy from my previous life means I can talk to most creatures that walk or fly, and a couple of those that swim like me well enough to push me to shore, whether I want to go there or not.

My companions always notice that I heal quicker than them. A few have noticed I heal even quicker when killing things. A couple of them noticed I can ask blazes to let me pass. It seems that a scion of Firecrag retains the love of the Eternal Fires no matter where he is.

Many who notice join my free company. Strangely, not one who has seen what I can do has betrayed me. Even the ones who live to retire while I continue to lead, untouched by time - except in the skills I have honed for longer than any.

"Major. You with us?"

I grin.

"Got nowhere else to be tonight, Bex. What's on the menu?"

"Terrorist hangout, one high-value target. You know how this goes."

"Where do I meet our local hires?"

She gestures towards the lights of the compound about a kilometre off.

"There's a bridge across a stream. They're a hundred metres west along the watercourse, same side as the compound."

"Good enough. You know the routine."

We exchange nods and she's gone, her stealth gear good enough to baffle my sensors after a couple of metres. I head out to join tonight's wrecking ball.

The nine mercenaries are very good. We're inside the main building before the last of them falls at my feet.

"Well, now. Looks like we've got you at last, Ruben Eternal."

The thickly-accented voice seems to come from the air itself, but it doesn't matter. Every now and then, some mob or other will realise what I represent and try to capture me. Thing is, stories about immortal warriors predate their efforts, and I've read them all.

The EMP flatlines everything electric for a mile or so. The MK79 fire bomb that follows is antique, but effective. Bex got a couple of containers of them cheap. The missiles and launcher were even cheaper. Old weapons have finally become subject to fashion. Which means we can cheaply arm up with all sorts of unpleasantness that modern warriors are ill-prepared for.

It takes me a while, but eventually the flames part to reveal the ugly bird we use for getting in and out of places without attracting attention.

I walk from the conflagration, brushing flakes of clothing from myself as I jog across to board the angular VTOL. I get given several thumbs up as I scramble in.

Bex grins as she hands me a pair of shorts.

"We got their local command, too. They were nearly up to the job."

I laugh.

"But only nearly."

Good. Might get a few years of peace and quiet this time.

"Up, up, and away. Tonight's victuals are on me. Which brings me to the key question: where are we celebrating tonight?"

Chafni shouts across.

"Little place in Tajikistan. My uncle's brother married a local woman and they opened it a few years back. They keep hassling my folks about me coming to visit. Bringing you lot along will serve them right for being so pushy."

Proximity Causes

"We all call it 'safe space'. The inventors of the concept called it 'social distancing'. It was only two metres back then. They used it, along with increased ventilation and personal masking, to slow some respiratory epidemics. Sociologists still argue about the long-term effects on everything except health. But, I digress. Which is something you'll get used to it if you choose to enrol in this course."

The scruffy woman standing by the lectern looks out at the packed hall. Standing room only. Every person verified to be in good health by the scanners at the entrance to the venue. She knows more than half of the attendees are here simply because it's an authorised proximity gathering. They just want to feel a crowd about them.

"So, here you all are, crammed in like venues used to able to do all the time. No screens, no grids, just a mob and a speaker. I know many of you don't really care about what I have to say."

She sees rapid movement. The security team is pushing through the crowd towards the front. With a swift double blink she drops monitoring lenses over her eyes.

There! Third row back, next to the aisle. A seated body is already at ambient temperature.

"Okay, folks. We have a little situation and I need you to do what I say. This is a Compliance Directive for the entire Grantham Hall Complex."

That gets their attention. CDs are instant emergency laws, applicable for no more than four hours, and only for clearly delineated areas.

"Everybody standing, please stay where you are. I know it's going to be difficult, but please do so with a minimum of moving about."

Liaden, the security lead, reaches the figure. He quickly checks the body, then looks her way and nods.

"Your attention, please. Looks like we've had a narcodeath. Please follow the instructions of our security personnel and you'll be on your way in no time. Tonight's presentation will be rescheduled."

She sees accepting shrugs and resigned looks. Overdoses and poisonings from self-medication with black market pharmaceuticals are on the rise. You only get advice for free from the NHS, and dealers are always ready to peddle cheap remedies.

It's a bitter irony. NHS sites and lines are always busy. Medical personnel in other countries contact them when they need accurate recommendations. Treatment advice that often results in deaths here frequently saves lives abroad.

Tonight, the drugs are actually beneficial. A useful cover, because a body gone cold that fast has been drained.

Pholmor have lived among human populations for millennia. After learning how to rein in their constant hunger so they didn't grow to outlandish sizes, they just blended in, faded from history, and then from mythology.

They are the precursors of vampires, succubi, incubi - and every other legendary thing that steals life from humans - feeding via an energy transfer that only needs skin to skin contact. They can consume everything we do, but their rudimentary digestive systems extract no nutrients. They sustain themselves by bleeding energy from us.

The prodigious sizes they used to attain were due to the need to store the excess energy acquired while satiating their prodigious appetites. It gave them the reserves to go without prey for long periods, but had the drawback of making them obvious.

Finding them isn't easy. The usual way is like tonight. For anyone weakened by illness or another condition, an unexpected loss of vitality can kill.

A scuffle breaks out. There's the crackle of a suppressor, followed by an inhuman scream that makes heads turn. Another Pholmor for the fenced valley below the research centre in the Scottish Highlands.

"Please stay calm and co-operate, folks. There's no reason to get excited."

Not tonight, anyway.

When exactly Pholmor were shifted from myth to concealed fact remains classified information. The authorities keep their existence secret in fear of the number of erroneous killings that would occur should they ever be revealed. Accusations, paranoia, witch hunts, and lynch mobs – it's hideous to contemplate.

Scores

I'm free of traffic and clear of the city. Time to open this beastie up. I press the accelerator and the response is like a gigantic hand pressing my body into the seat. In the stowage space I hear bullion smashing into the boxes of gems and jewellery. Must remember to check under the carpets when I empty out.

"Unidentified perpetrator, northbound on the **MM2** hyperway. Stop now or we will deploy countermeasures that may endanger your life."

Having just stolen treasures worth over a billion, I'm surprised there aren't missiles chasing me down the road already. My guess is they don't want to explosively scatter the goods. Can't have some heirloom being found by a down-and-out from the sticks. Wouldn't be right.

"Unidentified perpetrator. We are-"

I tap for two-way.

"The name's Nat."

There's a pause. One-nil.

"I thank you. Okay, Nat. You should know this road is screened on both sides to a height of eight metres, and the baffles mean ten metres either side are impassable for unshielded lifeforms. That racer can't ram through the screens, so you're effectively on rails until you hit the waypoint at Leeds."

I was hoping they'd rely on the installations rather than go for something ad-hoc.

"Big junction there. I could skate a lane or two."

"No, Nat. Air units have already closed those options off. Your rocket pack won't have the thrust to get you far enough to evade us."

So they noticed.

"Somebody deserves an award for spotting that, officer."

Another pause. Two-nil.

"Thank you, Nat. I'll mention it, but my boss doesn't look happy enough. If I could get you to pull over, that might do it."

There's no attempt to stop me as the curves around Birmingham go by, even when I drop under 300kph to negotiate the last S-bend. They really think the security fortress at Leeds is going to do it. Only two on-ramps between me and there, and I'm too fast for conventional rolling roadblocks.

"How's your fuel, Nat? You've been running overboost for a while."

"What makes you think I'm overboosting?"

"That's a Trefoil 4 with the aftermarket Sprinter conversion. Looks well done, but the consumption at the top end is phenomenal. It's why they went bust: they couldn't fix the power drain problem."

The police lady is a gearhead. Surprise. Two-one.

"A gearhead in uniform? Never thought that would happen."

Is that a little laugh?

"Nor did I, but a career is a career, and they're rare these days. Speaking of which, yours is soon to be over. Why not pull over and we can talk Trefoils?"

"You have one?"

"Sprinter body on top, stock Trefoil 3 underneath."

"So that's how you knew."

"Nat, my boss says that at this speed, you've got about thirty minutes before you smash into the barriers at Leeds. He'd like you to take my offer, says we can talk while they organise retrieval and arrest, but he's also arranged for clean-up crews at Leeds. Says the choice is yours."

"That's kind of him. So, what's your name, gearlady?"

"Constable Tuhina O'Conner. What now, Nat?"

My skyscan flashes green.

"I fixed the power drain problem on the Sprinter conversion."

"How?"

"The Sprinter fastback gives enough room to plumb in a Ceres-Class gravitic core."

Pause. Three-one.

I pull the stick back and the beastie unsticks like **1000**kph is nothing and space is where it wants to be.

"Blow your boss a kiss from me, Tuhina. Chat again next heist."

"The rocket pack casing conceals your environment module? Clever. Catch you next heist."

Good comeback. Three-two, and on for a rematch.

Warnings

The cargo bay seems deserted. It should be packed. We know someone performed a 'war action' here. They overrode emergency reseal functions and warning routines, closed off internal access, then dropped the environment fields. We don't know why. Also, the venting of the bay was actioned from inside. That's the detail that bothers me: somebody probably killed themselves to do this.

"Mikey Four, this is Pattison. We've secured all the dumped ships. They'd all been locked in unsealed states nine hours before the bay was vented."

Colson chuckles.

"This ride has left weird and is headed toward menacing."

He's right.

"Too true, partner."

The lights come on. The place is a typical cargo bay, in regulation shades of pale blue or grey. Except for the copious amounts of red daubed across the floor and up the walls to about twice human height.

I gesture to the décor.

"Welcome to menacing."

He turns completely about.

"Pattison, this is Colson One. Please inspect dumped ships for unusual markings."

"Colson One, this is Pattison. Was about to call. Looks like some of these ships hosted bloodbaths. Savah, our Dadil

Huntswoman, tells me the spatter patterns are right for a large predator slaughtering human-sized prey."

All vessels and stations have Giger's Alien on their safety displays. Any form of new infestation could do for us all. His creation encourages paranoid proaction.

"Where are the bodies?"

Colson has a point. I don't want to be the one to answer, but he and I are first-in recon. It's our job.

With Savah's analysis in mind, I set the forensic reconstruction to 'track' the massacre from the traces. Four drones flit from my backpack. Now to find something to do while the process completes.

Turning around, I see Colson standing in the centre of the bay. He's motionless. I jog over to him.

"What's up?"

He doesn't reply. I see his head is back, like he's looking at the ceiling above. I move round so I can see into the same section.

"You see?"

His whisper is my saving grace. I shake my head and put a hand on his shoulder.

"Yes. It's not DSHS."

'Deep Space Hallucinatory Syndrome' can happen to any human spacer without warning. There's no cure except to get, and stay, planetside.

"That's all of them, isn't it?"

I set off a Mass Casualty Alert. It lets those who come next prepare, and gives me access to additional routines. Looking up at the tangle of bodies and hull sealant, I wait.

294. All personnel, minus one...

"Last one triggered the venting. Let's go find them."

She's in the dented emergency control room. Barricaded the door, patched herself up, then dragged the needed kit onto the floor rather than trying to stand one-legged.

"Her name was Siobhan O'Malley. There's a note scrawled on the wall: 'Never seen the like. Tripeds in body armour. Two clawed arms on the right, giant pincer on the left. Disabled our systems before making entry. Hope the one that got my leg goes with this bay.'"

Entry!

"Code Red, all units. This is Mikey Four. Check all ingress points for unrecognised traffic. Shoot first."

The silence lasts for five minutes.

"Mikey Four, this is Pattison. Ventral lock records an unidentified docking nine hours prior to venting. It departed four minutes after we arrived in-system. Residuals indicate it probably exited near L5."

We entered at L4.

"Relay a Code Red to everything within range: 'New hostile sentients. Technically advanced, stealthy, very capable, and lethal.'"

Colson adds: "Likely they've struck before."

True. But now we know.

Thank you, Siobhan.

Sad Songs

The world burned. Several places only did so until they sank. Congregations sang paeans to the skies, the fires, the waters, or the earth. The rest of us listened to what we had while we could. All of us heard the songs coming from distant hills or the clouds above, songs we knew told of melancholy, but never had words we could relate.

I started off riding through the apocalypse in a convoy, sent to help a town defend itself from a rising river and an end-of-days militia. By the time we got there, the townsfolk were screaming like animals as they set the surviving militia on fire one by one.

Our chief got himself gutted trying to control the situation. Then Sergeant Jones recognised one of the militia, and things went the way you'd expect. When the shooting stopped, all the screamers were dead. To our surprise, both townsfolk and a militia emerged from hiding.

We were all at a loss for what to do next when the river made a concerted attempt to drown us all. Those who escaped listened to the news, saw the signs in the sky – not all man-made – and decided to become a tribe.

Eleven winters is all it took for me to go from soldier, to tribesman, to pack leader, and finally: sole survivor. In the five winters since then, I've seen many things I can't explain, and survived more by luck than judgement.

I usually avoid supernaturals. Most of them are very, very unhappy with humans. I get the feeling they're trying to fix our busted planet, which includes killing us to make sure we never get a chance to break it again.

But there's something about the winged figure on that hill...

A hard slog to get up here, but it's worth it to stand in the heat emanating from it. Not even the winter winds dare disturb this one. I join it in looking down at the choppy sea. Skeletal vehicles and dead hedgerows protrude from the shallow waters. I glance sideways. It's sitting on a broken bench.

Curiosity triumphs over fear.

"What was this place?"

Ruby eyes regard me. I see that tears have left scald marks from eyes to chin.

"They used to call it Mount Caburn. On winter nights they would gather fallen yew branches to make ritual fires."

There is no menace to this being. I've fled from many who were more threatening... And less dangerous. So powerful, too calm. Running would be futile.

But... I know what he's doing.

"A vigil? Why bother?"

He smiles.

"I've talked to many powers during my time down here. I came to realise humanity had become a force none of us could rein in. We, the chosen, set above the wiles of mortals by groups of mortals needing objects to venerate - or seeking excuses to condemn - were nothing but sideshows."

"You cry for us?"

His laughter is like a body blow. I collapse to my knees.

"Never. Every winter solstice I keep vigil for those who followed me down. I told Him that humanity should end because

27

man would always ruin Eden, no matter how big He made it. His reply banished me."

I know this angel.

"Fundamental truths are rarely welcomed, especially by the powerful."

He nods.

Taking a seat on the other bit of bench, I dig out my last two cans of beer and offer one to him.

"Really?"

"Drink it before it gets warm, Lucifer."

He chuckles.

The fallen angel and an old soldier, keeping watch through the longest night...

Hosanna, for what it's worth.

Red Boat, Blue Boat

The camera view wobbles, then stabilises. The blurry picture goes from blotches of colour to a woman's face against a backdrop of ruddy foliage. Gloria smiles cheerfully, her expression not betraying her jaded thoughts: another week, another backwater, another boring tourist information recording.

Wilf, the cameraman, raises a thumb for her to start.

"Welcome to Tashtaun, ladies and gentlemen. We're here today to witness the Red Boat Festival, a spectacle that stems from a merging of the memory of the arrival of the first Earth colonists with local legends about liberators from the stars. While it has echoes of the old cargo cults of Earth, it remains a unique side-effect amongst Earth's interstellar colonisation efforts."

Turning to her left, she nods politely to the squat, furry, hippo-headed biped standing there.

"This is Taklakak, Sturom of the local Collective, which is the equivalent of a mayor who controls a city council."

"*Modo modeo.*" Taklakak nods.

The woman looks confused and glances off to her right.

"Cliff? I thought he spoke Glish?"

A voice from off screen replies.

"No, there's an interpreter. Radkaku. He's standing behind Wilf."

The 'u' suffix means he's 'enlightened', whatever that means.

She leans sideways and beckons. Another hippo-headed being steps into view.

Radkaku steps up and gives a wide, toothy grin.

Gloria nods towards Taklakak.

"What did he say?"

The two beings exchange a flurry of sounds. Radkaku turns to Gloria.

"He wonders if you need him anymore because he needs to get back to arranging the braids for the gathering."

"He said all that in two words?"

"No, he just told me that. What he said to you was a greeting between owner and servitor."

"I don't own him."

"I know. He thinks he owns you."

"What?"

Radkaku shrugs.

"If you're not born on Tashtaun, you're something from the stars. Anything from the stars belongs to whoever finds it or whoever it first talks to. To this unenlightened Tashtaun, you're nothing but a talking meteorite."

"I still don't understand."

"We had ancient legends of benefactors from the stars. Then humans came from the stars and improved life for all Tashtauns. We wanted something to make life better. You did. That makes you useful. We put up with your silly behaviour because of that."

"Silly?"

"Like this, where you take pictures of the Red Boat Victory Gathering while passing the cause off as a hybrid between our myths and memories of your arrival."

"Why is that silly?"

"Because of your assumption of superiority. You came down and gave us many gifts, allowed us to travel to other planets, helped us establish trade routes - and taught us how to do that ridiculous tourism thing.

"To us, lavishing gifts on another tribe before a war is fought is a sign of weakness. How we see it is that you came to make offerings. Unenlightened Tashtaun are happy to accept your worship."

"So we fly through space, and command science you cannot comprehend, alongside weapons of unimaginable power, yet are your inferiors?"

"Yes. You did not conquer. You asked politely. We were too surprised to make war on you."

Gloria looks confused.

"But the boats. You were wandering. Our ship landing guided you to shore. That first collective built the human enclave at Skriddyon. The studies show how that was such a pivotal event, how your lore shows that humanity saved the Tashtaun from extinction and assisted them back to civilisation."

The interpreter shakes his head, then gestures for Taklakak to leave. He waits until the Sturom is out of hearing range.

"The Tashtaun you landed near were just one tribe: The Second Red. They were relocating due to a family split, where one tribe becomes two because it's grown too big. You landed on the spawning ground of a rival tribe, the Third Blue. Your giant red boat scorched the blue nests to nothing and killed all their Venerated. The surviving blue surrendered. It was a great victory for you. We expected to be set upon too, but you emerged from your boat and behaved like ones defeated, talking and making offerings. It confused us. Gradually we came to understand that had you decided to set down nine klim toward the dawn, you would have destroyed the red nests. Your actions had been nothing but chance. We chose to leave that truth out of record of the event. Likewise the fact that if you had destroyed the red nests and thus given victory to the Third

Blue, we would have made war against you for betraying what we perceived as a red heritage.

"Enlightened Tashtaun know the colour of your boats were, and are, irrelevant to our point of view. Unenlightened do not. It is why there are four hundred Red tribes, but only ninety Blue tribes that struggle daily for the means to exist."

Gloria raises her hand.

"What about all the studies?"

Radkaku smiles.

"We have special historical records for humans to examine. They're abbreviated and adjusted. Now, if you'll excuse me."

He walks quickly away.

Gloria calls after him: "Radkaku."

Looking surprised, he walks back.

"Why tell us?"

He smiles.

"I was deemed pleasing enough to be adopted into a Red family of notable standing. Before that, back to before the time of the Red Boat Disaster, my bloodline is Third Blue. I promised my ancestors I would take the insult of adoption and turn it to an advantage. This strikes me as a good way to break the ruling lie that ruins the lives of so many you never see."

Without waiting for further comment or question, he leaves.

Cliffy had wandered over to stand by Wilf.

"Folks, this one's not going to be 'cast. I'll send it to the Earth Alien Embassy for Tashtaun. After that, we are out of here."

Wilf nods.

"There's going to be some embarrassment. I have to wonder if the reason why that Tashtauni told us this is true."

Cliffy turns to him.

"I don't think it'll matter when it comes out, and it will. I do think we need to be a long way off by then. I've never been one for 'no witnesses' conspiracies, but erring on the side of caution seems good. So we're going. Now."

Gloria slips her wig off to reveal a crew cut.

"I'll have the ship ready to lift in twenty."

Wilf gives her a thumbs up.

"I'll have orbital clearances and registered jump co-ordinates in ten."

Cliffy turns to him.

"Make two sets of jump co-ordinates. Register one set, then forget about it. We'll be using the set you don't register."

They rush about.

Wilf winks at Gloria.

"You're not bored anymore, are you?"

She grins.

Via Tenebrae

We spent a century looking for life on other worlds. Found some, too. Most of it wasn't happy to meet us. Us being us, we got round that with our usual bonhomie and genocidal violence. Until we met the Pesserac. They kicked our murderous fleets clean out of space, and eradicated every colony we'd established through force. Then they politely informed us that peaceful colonisation was welcome, because we had a lot to offer. However, until we evidenced the 'fundamental societal changes' needed, we were also banned from participating in interstellar trading or receiving aid.

We were a pariah race. Despite the clear warnings, we often pushed our luck. They had clearly dealt with our kind before, and fallen foul of the lies told. We never had any survivors from attempts to break free of our restrictions.

It took Earth a century to sort itself out. Afterwards, things generally went well when we ventured into space. Then the first ship with cordallium-windowed viewing galleries journeyed into the long night and humanity discovered a reason to behave, and to believe. It swiftly became inconceivable for any to cause denial of access to this wonder.

"Ma'am. They're here."

Streamers of light twist past the gallery windows. Tourists crane their necks to try and see ahead. There's some pushing and shoving.

"Stand easy, people. You'll see them soon."

As if on cue, a whirl of colours comes to a halt by the largest window. It presses close. People step back. They can't help it. I couldn't, and I've seen this countless times.

In proximity to the pane, the colours part to reveal the outline of a figure. Completely negative, no reflections, nothing. Just a rainbow aura about a darkness that comes in varying shapes.

"Marla."

A man on my left sobs the name and collapses. Every time, with no exceptions, a revealed form will match someone's recollection of a lost loved one. It works with animals, too. Not that all animals can express grief or distinguish individuals, but recognition behaviour, pack calls and the like have forced the acknowledgement of this phenomenon.

Another whirling form presses close. A shorter, more rounded figure. A family to my right clutch each other tighter and burst into tears together.

The eerie event continues. So many people come each time. Most don't get the encounter they hope for, but all of them see enough to be convinced.

These things are like dolphins, riding ahead of our ships, shedding ribbons of light. How long they'd done this before we could see outside bare-eyed, we don't know. We can't detect them in any other way than with human sight. Several scientists I know surmise it's actually some interpretive quirk of the way our brains process light after it passes through cordallium crystal.

This new field of science is inconclusive and ongoing, but people don't care. The entities, or effects, or whatever they actually are, have been named 'Delphine' in some strange hybridisation of religion and perceived characteristics.

A faster-spinning mass of light presses to the window near me. The outline of my sister quirks her head in the way she used to do. It straightens up and, just before it whirls away, I swear there's a flash of light like the edge of a silver eyelid closing in a quick wink.

Every time I see this, I'm sure it's somehow learning from me how to represent her. My suspicions about that sort of behaviour have been dismissed so many times I've given up.

Much as I can't stop myself visiting, I'm increasingly convinced we're missing something. I've no idea what. But, in the moments before I sleep, it scares me.

New Friends

"A different feeling since you've been gone." Yeah, that's it. Too many times I catch myself looking down and back, only to find some scrub looking horrified, or empty air where one should be. They run off more often than they stay. People say it's difficult for them. What about me?

"Ten, left."

This one has a different feel. She's got this lilt to her voice. Fluent in some old language, too. Well, at least in what I guess is the swearing. Yet, when we're in the thick of it, her accent disappears. Just this monotone that delivers what I need, when I need it.

"Seven, centre."

Incoming. I rest my assault rifle against a building, taking the essential pause to make sure the building can take the weight, then crouch down, wind my arms back, preload my pectorals, and wait.

"Five, centre."

I glance back.

"Take three steps left, miss."

"Call me Riley."

"I'm Olaf."

She nods, then moves as instructed.

"Two, square."

It's coming right at me.

The shadow of wings flashes over us and I unwind, my arms swinging in so fast the air screams. I time it perfectly. The Gakdarbu is where it needs to be. My fists land on either side of its tubular head like gigantic hammers. Brutally effective: even if I get it wrong, I'll stun it, maybe paralyse it.

I get it right. The skull compresses, then explodes. Purple brains, green flesh and pink blood spray everywhere as shards of black bone strafe the area like a warm rain of obsidian daggers.

Amazing mess. So pret-

Something slams into the back of my left knee. I stagger that way and the hurtling body only clips my shoulder, instead of hitting me square in the chest. Even that love tap knocks me flat. I might be a bioengineered war giant, but taking five thousand kilos of headless alien raptor dead centre will spread me like chunky salsa.

There's a lot of that incomprehensible swearing. I hear her take a huge breath, let it out, then something pounds on the side of my calf.

"Do you pause to watch the rain of bloody shite every time, or do you only indulge when it's likely to get you killed, Olaf?"

I look down. She's pinned under my leg, beating on my calf armour with the butt of a pistol. I can see sparks where her impact field is having trouble keeping my leg from squashing her like a bug. Looking closer, I see her right shoulder is dented, and lower than it should be.

"You tackled me?"

"Yes, you gigantic idjit. Can't have you dying on my first day as your spotter. Now could you puh-leeze get the feck offa me?"

Oh, yeah. I move my leg.

"You need something for that shoulder?"

She nods, rolls to her knees, and shucks the shoulder plate.

"I need you to straighten that while I deal with my wandering joint."

Grabbing her right arm, she twists it, and then slams her right shoulder into my calf armour. There's a wet 'pop'. I feel a little sick. She screams.

I pick the armour plate up and carefully squeeze it back to true, then offer it to her.

She wipes her eyes and takes it. After locking it back into place, she grins.

"Nice job."

"What next?"

"At least being nearly crushed kept me mostly free of shite. There's a lake over in what used to be the city park. Wanna rinse?"

"Good idea, Riley."

"Too right it is. I'm stinky. You reek."

What? I take a deep breath and get a whiff of myself. Oof. The lady holding her nose and laughing at my expression has a point.

I like her.

Romeo and Julius

The mist-shrouded marsh is spotted with steaming pools of purple liquid, which, unlike the mud, won't grip you like glue. It'll either wash the blue-black slime from your boots, or you'll disappear into it, never to be seen again. Some say the pools are the traps of an unknown ambush predator. Others use terms like 'sinkhole' and 'bottomless'.

Through the hushed gloom, two figures move. The one in the lead strides slowly, letting powered armour take the strain while sensors probe the marshland ahead. The one behind moves with exaggerated sneaking movements, like some pantomime villain.

"'Romeo, Romeo-'"

The lead figure spins and points the arm without a mounted blaster at the other figure.

"Cut it out, Shakespeare."

"The name's Bond. Julius Bond."

"You keep saying that. I presume there's some antiquated pun value I'm fortunate enough to be ignorant of?"

Julius relaxes from his one-foot-raised comedic freeze and sighs theatrically.

"You're ignorant of our noble heritage, Captain Cadava. Cultural icons are how the future is shaped."

Romeo chuckles.

"That explains why each mission improves the ratings of whichever political leader got the most leverage at the previous strategy meeting, rather than achieving any objective that might end the fighting." He waves his arm about: "I used to call this place home. Now the province I grew up in is nothing but radioactive dirt, and the rest of the planet isn't much better."

"You lived around here?"

"Born next to the River Adissa. Lived there until I had to join up. I hunted through marshes like this when they were small enough to have their own names."

"Galley rumour says you're a conscript?"

"Close. I'm a signee. My choices were life imprisonment or service in the Consolidated Forces."

Julius stops next to Romeo.

"That's the murderer's gamble, Captain. What did you do?"

"I fell in lust. It ended badly."

"'Badly' is never speaking to your ex, maybe even getting beaten up by her relatives. I'm pretty sure killing doesn't feature."

Romeo looks up at the sky.

"Her name was Ivlietta. Real case of lust at first sight. Her cousin objected, my best friend challenged, then died when the cousin cheated. He got let off because the official witness lied.

"After spending a night with her, I got wounded killing the cousin: he ambushed me as I left her parent's house. She blackmailed the family doctor into treating me. The nurse betrayed us.

"I killed a close friend of hers when he tried to be hero and stop us escaping. That tore it all down. She called the law, but still cried like a baby as they led me away. Got the nurse blackballed, too."

Julius spreads his hands.

"Sorry I asked. Returning must be difficult."

Romeo shakes his head and points towards their target.

"The Escalusian forces on this planet are led by a local: General Laurence Mantua. He used to be a priest."

Julius slots a blaster into his arm mount and moves round to check Romeo's missile rack.

"Did he also used to be a registered witness who invigilated duels?"

Romeo chuckles, then steps behind Julius to check his missile rack.

"Good guess."

Julius laughs.

"Then I have to ask: 'wherefore art thou, Romeo?'"

"About to rain hell down upon that lying friar, Julius."

"'But, soft, what light through yonder window breaks?'"

"That'll be two flights of Sirius DK614 missiles."

"Then let us go 'wisely and slow'."

Romeo barks a short laugh before replying: "Indeed. 'They stumble that run fast.'"

Through the hushed gloom, two figures move with quiet purpose, violent delights in mind.

Witch Hunts

I didn't want to write this, but here's the thing: I have to.

Sitting in my study, looking out the window at a glorious sunny day, with kids running riot in the playground and old folk sat on benches watching the world go by, it's what many would call perfect.

Which is the root of my quandary. It's the 22nd July 1952. How can I tell them it's not going to last? The wondrous future of leisure supported by advanced technology that everyone talks about is a lie. I've seen it: the computers, the prosperity, the inequality, the Nazi trappings. For the majority of people, it's a dystopian 'work until you die' future, and it's less than a century away!

The machine doesn't have the ability to let me see how we get there. In truth, getting the view I have was a miraculous accident. Einstein had some ideas about the future being set, and viewable. I might have confirmed some of them.

What puzzled me is that what I see changes each time. Initially I thought it was because my act of viewing enacted some Heisenberg effect, then I thought it because of me viewing on different days – which may have some bearing, I admit.

The best explanation I have arrived at is a mix of Observer effect and some variant of the Grandfather paradox, either due to my observations, or possibly knowledge of what I have done and seen becoming public before it would have.

That stated, I am now more of the opinion that Einstein's fixed universe view is not entirely correct. I believe the view changes each time because I am seeing the various possible futures that could exist at that point, depending on which significant events transpire or fail between now and 2042.

My greatest horror is that not one of the futures I've seen differs in the fundamental composition of society. After all the sacrifices of the last decade, it seems the fascists will eventually triumph. The uniforms may differ, but the words, the hatred, the cowed populations and ruling elite are unmistakable.

I intend to continue to document my work for a few more days, then prepare an initia

The man finishes reading, then reaches over the body to pull the page from the typewriter. He turns to the woman who is rummaging through the cluttered bookshelves that cover two walls of this small study.

"No need. The whole place will have to go. We can't afford to miss a thing."

"Thank God."

She drops the papers in her hand with a sigh of relief, then waves to indicate the room.

"Is it that serious?"

"From what I just read, he's a dyed-in-the-wool communist crank. Looks like another scientist driven doolally by his work."

"Senator McCarthy might be overstating, but he's not wrong. I'm beginning to wonder if all this science is such a good thing, either."

He turns and pretends to check outside the window so she doesn't see his smile. Turning back, he pulls out a lighter. She opens a slim silver case, extracts a pair of cigarettes, and puts both between her lips. He lights them. Then, with a little flourish, he sets fire to the page and drops it on the floor.

They step out of the room as the fire starts to spread. He takes the cigarette she holds out. After waiting long enough to be sure the place is well alight, they leave. Walking a short way down the road, they duck into a black DeSoto and drive off.

Wolf Now

"My father was outraged when they switched the banners to holograms."

"Why? Saves labour, and is far more hygienic."

"He mentioned something about heritage needing physical presence to root it."

"Videos of this tunnel over the years show it better. Fans can see this place from wherever they are."

"That was part of his point. Accessing it so easily cheapens the emotional tie, or something like that."

"For older generations, I'd agree. But for those born and raised in the digital world, our nostalgia is just a few clicks away."

"He had a big problem with that, too. Something about memory filtering emotional content over time: what's important are the memories that remain. If the moments are always available, you frequently never get to work through and settle the associated emotions, be they good or bad."

"I think I understand. Well, on an intellectual level. To understand it emotionally, I'd have to delete a lot... No, that wouldn't be right. To do it properly, I'd need to grow up with the need to retain moments because they aren't captured in, or cued by, hundreds of image prompts."

"That's deep."

"Not really. He was a man who only had an organic mind to use. Only a few steps from the wolf now."

"'Wolf now'?"

"No detailed memories; no real comprehension of the passage of time."

"Is that such a bad thing?"

"Actually, now that you mention it: no."

The Specimen

The room is unadorned. No evidence of tooling; not even a scuff mark mars the bare rock. No dust, no insects. Nothing moves. This place is still. It's uncanny. Unnerving for some.

Jeffrey Palist found it fascinating. He wiped himself down with a deliberation that bordered on reverence before stepping into the room. Taking the few steps across the downward-sloping rock surround, he walked out onto the yellow-striped grass until he stood at the centre of the room.

Fortunately, he left his drone camera on. The recording shows him turning around, clearly looking for something. He spread his hands, uttered the words "I can't see you", and dropped dead.

The rescue team didn't even make it to his body. They each took three steps onto the grass and died. The second team were dressed in biohazard suits and found all organic materials on the first team had desiccated to the point of crumbling when touched.

Jeffrey's body wasn't desiccated. It looked like it was melting: slowly seeping into the pale earth. Any striped grass that protruded from the liquid mess was quivering.

A decision was made to leave everything in place until further research could occur. The second team were on their way back when they too dropped dead.

Six days later, beautiful flowers bloomed amidst the remains. Metallic purple, glacier blue, blood red, and snow white. Petals arranged around pistils that resembled jade green compound eyes, with no visible stamens.

Five days after that, the petals drifted down and shattered. The compound 'eyes' were revealed to be shells, from which golden worms hatched. Those asymmetrical horrors opened rings of glossy black eyes and wriggled toward the exit. People were still panicking when Sarah Simpson noticed they were dying while ascending the rock surround. They shrivelled as they went, falling apart while struggling up the slope to escape. The pieces rolled back and sank into the pale earth.

Nineteen years later, Sarah stands next to me as we watch another batch of worms die.

"So the amount of material only affects the number of worms, not their size?"

She nods.

"The worms are all the same length, give or take a millimetre or two. None of them are more than two centimetres wide. A hundred kilos of animate organics will create twenty. A hundred kilos of inanimate organics, four. Blooming and hatching periods never change. The grass never exceeds eight centimetres in height, and is shorter toward the edges of the container."

"Container?"

"We've monitored this thing for nearly two decades. The room is precisely designed to keep it alive, but nearly dormant: dependant on prey wandering in. The rock surround emits radiation whenever living material comes into direct contact. The worms are killed by a gamma burst that never goes further than thirty millimetres from the rock.

"This whole edifice is largely impervious to penetrative scanning. What we've found is baffling: indications that the interior of the rock sometimes exhibits liquid properties. Scanning the grass reveals a hemisphere of living material, flat side about five centimetres below the surface. It's nearly fills the container. All gaps between hemisphere and rock are filled with the same dirt the grass grows from."

She turns to look at me, gesturing in the direction of the room.

"This place was designed to keep the hatchery alive, but to never allow the hatchlings out."

"You're trying to find out why whoever built this place didn't just kill the thing, and you don't believe any of the 'religious cult' or similar theories?"

Sarah nods.

"Welcome aboard. We could be at this for a very long time."

Mischief

They warn us about culture clashes, especially the dangers of exposing primitive cultures to advanced technology. My mother went with the concept of "one being's magic is another being's science". Ever since, if our devices are too much for the locals, we present ourselves as sorcerers or shamans hired to protect a merchant. It's stupidly effective, too. Fireworks and hologram projectors have saved my life more times than weapons and violence.

I remember her telling me that Fiona seemed more fairy than petite low-gravity worlder. Said she had a talent for mischief. Tonight, I'm probably going to have to intervene, but the mischief is gold standard.

The hulking barbarian points to the media box in her hand.

"Does making the lights go out kill the little men in the relic?"

"Yes, but not the little women. They fall into an enchanted sleep until you make the lights come on again. Then they conjure the ghosts of their favourite men back to life so they can cavort with them some more."

"They are comely lasses. How does one take service with them?"

"Surely you don't want to limit your adventuring spirit by living a life of leisure in a little box full of women?"

"After the winter I've had? You can pour that adventuring spirit over your backside and light it."

Fiona flashes me a 'dug myself a hole' look.

I shrug, watch the look of panic cross her face, then grin.

Closing my eyes, I interface with V-space and get the Dragonfly to patch me through to our equatorial trading team.

"Tony! What's Fiona baited into a fury this time?"

I grimace.

"Nothing yet, Larsen, but her current plaything is nearly three metres across. He's some barbarian who does a guard boss thing during off seasons. Pretty good at both, judging by the quality of his gear."

"Part of his face got green tattoos?"

"At least half."

"That's a Drashtyn Battlemaster. Think medieval special forces with command skills."

"Man needs a job somewhere warm. Got anything?"

"We've a jolly merchant lamenting the lack of toughs to head up his next expedition. That do?"

"Tell him you can bring him a veteran Battlemaster from the northlands using our tame elemental. Providing he pays us full finder's price."

"Fiona going to puppet the barbarian?"

"Yup. He'll be oblivious to being flown in the Dragonfly. We'll tell him it was elemental magic; he'll be fine."

"Tasty. Peggy and Regan can fake a summoning to give you a landing zone."

"Perfect. See you tomorrow morning."

"We'll be ready. Come in on my beacon. Be sure to land inside the circle of flames."

"Got it."

I open my eyes. Fiona is sitting on an enormous knee, looking like a nervous pet. I stand and wave my tankard to get his attention.

"Battlemaster! Before you succumb to a Sprite's Bargain, I can offer you employ in Wishtar."

He comes up fast. Fiona rolls out of an untidy landing to tuck herself behind me.

"Gently, now. You know sprites can only do as their natures dictate."

The massive brow furrows.

"I'm aware, merchant. What's the job?"

"Trail lord for an expedition."

"I accept."

Fiona dashes forward and slaps a control rig in with a low blow. He stiffens, then jerkily walks from the tavern with her at his side.

She walks him all the way to the Dragonfly and lays him down in the cargo bay. He starts snoring immediately.

I grin.

"You need to work on the walking, but nicely done."

"We off to make money?"

"In the warm, too. Wishtar, here we come."

I Give the Guns

"You have to understand. He is an exemplar of all that is godless in our society. He and his ilk will lead us down the road to perdition."

I reached out and lifted his chin with a finger.

"What will you do afterwards?"

He looked confused.

"Afterwards?"

"There has to be a 'next'. So many dedicated men fail because of a lack of ambition."

I felt his trembling intensify.

"Carson. Reagan. McCartney. I'll go on to get all of them, God willing."

Such irony.

I gave him a gun.

"He's going to set them free! How can any decent man even consider such insanity? After all we stood for, after all we sacrificed and surrendered, I thought at least he wouldn't betray us like this."

I pushed the bottle his way. He nodded in thanks and refilled his glass.

"What will you do?"

"It's not will, it's an imperative. I must stop him to save the nation that will emerge from this hellish fight with itself."

"You have a plan?"

"He's at the theatre tomorrow night. He'll be vulnerable in small company. It's my best chance."

Petty ideals, but amusing.

I gave him a gun.

"Ilya says it's all a façade. He's going to drag the world into a war so terrible we may never survive. His own people know that. They've got some ex-marine set up to do it, but his position is useless. There's a spot by the Book Depository that would be ideal."

I nodded, as if I had some care as to his reasoning.

"And?"

"When their guy fires, I can get a better line and be gone while they hunt the source of the echo, which his shot is bound to do. They'll perjure themselves hiding the fact they couldn't catch the real assassin. Help me stop him. This guy is lying to the people."

The deceit was not where he thought it was.

That's when I gave him a gun.

"My homeland must be freed!"

Not drastic enough. I waited.

"Unification is the only way. We must have independence. The archduke has to go. In the chaos that follows, my people will win through."

That's what I wanted. His being young enough to avoid the death penalty was a bonus. Incarceration of such a famous radical could have spawned many useful things, had an event of the kind I sought to start not come to pass.

That's why I gave him a gun.

Those are my favourites. If ever there was a device more suited to evil, yet so often promoted as a tool for good, I have yet to find it. A gun will serve the backhand from on high. I am a being with wealth, refinement, and no need of introduction. My work is precision itself. The game is agreed: one man, one gun. One of the players I gift will bring down your lamentable civilisation.

Time - and firepower - are on my side.

On a Sunny Afternoon in Kentucky

The sign on the small shack reads 'Booth 7'. The gate next to it is a long steel pole with heavy chains hanging down.

The uniformed man looks unimpressed, in the way that gate guards have honed to perfection in the many centuries since guarding gates became a vocation.

"Department 51. Fifty... One? Like Area 51?"

The man sitting in the car blinks sweat from his eyes and sighs.

"Something like that."

"So you're here to see what the boys and girls brought in last night?"

The man in the car stops blinking. Sweat rolls across his glassy eyeballs as he stares at the guard.

"I wasn't aware of anything of significance being discovered where that aircraft came down, soldier."

The guard salutes. Another trait honed by gate guards since time immemorial is the ability to know, without question, when an odd-looking stranger trying to get in is actually so powerful he or she could bring all sorts of trouble down upon them.

"Sorry, sir. I'll still have to call it in, sir."

The man in the car nods.

The guard picks up the handset and punches a button.

"Colonel Edwards? Sayers, Booth Seven. I have someone from Department 51 demanding entry, sir."

He listens for a moment, then puts the phone down, steps out, and walks the gate open. The driver goes by without acknowledging him.

After closing the gate, he re-enters the booth. His partner looks up from the screen she'd been pretending to work at to avoid getting involved.

"Sounds like you dodged that right."

He heaves a sigh of relief, then raises a finger.

"Funny how the Colonel didn't ask for the bloke's name."

His partner pauses, then snatches the handset from the cradle.

"Line's dead."

They look at each other, grab their rifles, and dart round to the back of the booth.

"Where's the line go?"

"We're at the end of the spur that strings the booths together. It runs down to Booth 1, then to the base along the side of the main access road."

"You stay here."

He watches as she grubs in the earth until she pulls a cable into view. With a grin, she heads off along the fence, dirt spraying as the cable comes up. She disappears into the distance.

A fair while later, she comes sprinting back.

"The wire's been cut! Our end is spliced into a line that runs out towards the woods beyond the fence. Our radios are dead, too."

He grips his rifle tighter and looks about.

"What in tarnation is going on?"

The orange and blue flash of the base disappearing in a sphere of crackling energy is all the warning they get. She dives behind a weed-covered concrete divider left behind after resurfacing work on the road. He stands there and watches.

The blast tears him from his feet. His flailing form disappears over a low hill. She braces her back against the divider, willing it to hold. Heat sears exposed skin and chars clothing.

After what seems an age, she rolls to her knees and looks towards the base. A cigar-shaped turquoise object rises from the pall of smoke that shrouds what remains. It hovers, swings about, then accelerates away towards Edgewood.

She lifts her radio and switches it to a general military channel. It clicks and hisses reassuringly.

"Break-break. This is Private Mally Clarke at Camp Fitzgerald. Lone survivor, declaring security breach and disaster state. Emergency, emergency."

While waiting for the helicopters to arrive, she decides on what will be left out of any reports she makes.

Clearance

Emotional isn't something we're meant to be. Since losing the team, immersing myself in duty let me get by. Until I came here: this place makes it impossible to remain detached.

"How does it look, Baker Leader?"

This mission sickens me.

"I'm sitting on a half-kilometre jetty that's older than my grandmother, watching the lonely light of a moored yacht reflecting on waters so tranquil you'd think somebody painted them in."

"Don't go poetic on us, Baker Leader. Shalshelix is a resource world for humankind. It has to be neutralised."

"Boil the seas, salt the earth?"

"We're only going to ignite the atmosphere. There's no need to commit war crimes."

Good to know we're not going to be breaking any rules of engagement.

My team comm blinks. That's not right: my next mission is to build another Baker team. I switch channels.

"Baker Leader, receiving. Who is this?"

"Baker Seven."

Sendra?

"You're dead."

"The Hierarchs are wrong, Jastal. Humanity is worthy, just not completely martial. In that, they represent a huge threat: the danger of showing we Koekuld that there is another way."

"You're dead!"

"No. The human survivors of that ambush saved me. We spent eleven months holding half a corvette together before rescue found us."

"You always were more metalworker than warrior."

"Proud of it, too."

"Why now?"

"I don't want to see another world sterilised. Besides, I live here."

Carry on, betray, lose again? Decisions in the twilight. The water laps at my boots. I hear laughter coming from the yacht.

"How?"

"I need your vessel clearance code. The fireship is incoming. Nobody dies if we detonate it in the outer system."

The aftereffects would make it impossible for the fleet to remain... I smile. Choice made.

"KZXM2137FD401AC4."

Monsters of All Sizes

The little Albot skitters across the floor, legs not quite obeying its eager commands to leap onto Rhonda and pester her until she gives in and plays with it.

"Slow down, Saffy. You'll break a leg again."

"Shan't."

The tiny terror skids to a stop against her boot and promptly starts to climb, foreclaws doing the work while the rear legs bob like shiny pendulums with claws on.

"And what, young Albot, do you think you are?"

"Welociwaptor. Comin' to 'ill you."

Rhonda chuckles.

"Where did you get 'velociraptor' from, Saffy?"

"Wilm. Bwoosh lemme see. Juwassic Wuld."

It scrambles higher, oblivious to the look we exchange before shouting together.

"Bruce!"

We hear the sound of someone falling from a bunk two rooms down. The swearing continues for a while, then gets louder. Bleary eyes regard us from a tace nearly lost in shaggy hair and an even shaggier beard.

"What's burning?"

Rhonda points to the climber on her sweatshirt.

"Your credentials, again."

I push a chair towards Bruce.

"You showed it Jurassic World?"

He shrugs.

"She loved Jurassic Park so much, I couldn't say no."

Rhonda leans forward, her tone deceptively light.

"Which one?"

"She thought the beginning of The Lost World with the Compys on the beach was really funny, but she loved the velociraptors in JP3."

I watch as Rhonda turns red. I hear Bruce swallow. Time to head this off before it, which is doing that 'intense witnessing' process they do, gets some first-hand examples of emotions we'd rather it didn't get working examples of.

"I can see that being appropriate. It's meant to be a co-ordinating influence. Speaking of which, why don't you go and put it with Pack Zeta for a while?"

It cocks its head towards me, then leaps down and scampers across to Bruce, arms spread like a child running to a beloved uncle. He picks it up with a beaming smile, then exits the room chatting happily with it.

As their cheerful conversation fades, I turn back to catch Rhonda's look of concern.

"I think he'd make a marvellous handler."

She smiles.

"Thank you. I thought we were going to have to set up another hunt, because he's an awful behaviourist."

"His family ran a pet shop in Scunthorpe. He was a juggler. When things all fell in and the arts got side-lined, he somehow talked his way into a junior opening on the robotics program at Autonomous Warrior IV. Something about animal training at the pet shop and working with some of the early Sony dogbots. Anyway, ten years later, here he is. The sheer brass to do that has got to be worth something."

"If he can pass it on."

"He'll do it by example. You see how it's keen on him? He should be given a chance to have it as a live-in companion. It'll teach the packs. Make every pack before Zeta the control, Zeta and up get its influence."

She looks thoughtful.

"All well and good, but what's the fallback?"

I steeple my fingers.

"We decommission unit Sapphire-33, nickname 'Saffy', and have packs Alpha through Epsilon use Bruce for a hunt. Run it as urban stealth with body retrieval while he's on leave."

"That'll leave a lot of blood to explain."

"Animal rights stunt will cover it."

"What if he goes for publicity or aid?"

"The 77th can handle the media, and Security Team 4 already think Bruce is a waste of space."

"So they would run interference. That covers all bases. I like it. Good plan, Sergeant."

I snap her a casual salute.

"Thanks, Captain."

Revelation

"You're a killer, Jorn. What you're doing out here? Everybody whispers about it."

There's only so many precautions you can take when you're planning escape routes. Eventually, you will arrive somewhere others know you want to be.

"Why, matey? We were the finest special ops team. They used our missions as tutorials, man. Tutorials!"

Another fact of military life is that you spend your time hoping to meet soldiers who magnify your skills, and for you to do the same for them. The team gestalt is exhilarating. Betraying it is usually unforgivable. Right now, I'm hoping for a miracle.

"Jorn, mate: you're done. The rest of the company are scattered across this wasteland. I click once and they're headed this way, covering every escape option you can think of along the way."

Tino's already clicked. This is a delaying tactic. My record of escaping has started coming with bodycounts that make even hardened killers and their masters nervous. I see him quickly tap his belt. His comms have gone dark and he doesn't like it one bit. Give him his due, he doesn't show me anything other than that.

Time to try.

"Funny thing about Escalanza, Tino. How we had so many go off mission and never understood why?"

"They stopped enquiries after you vanished." He snaps his fingers. "You found out!"

Four years. It's taken him four years, and confronting me, to make that connection.

"What do you know about the Nineteen Realms, Tino?"

"All the magic crap from kiddy cartoons and fantasy books rolled into a comfy blanky for tree-huggers, headcases, and cowards."

There's the heart of the problem. The revelation about the faerie worlds sent mankind into a collective epiphany of denial. Decades later, they're still trying to erase the hated reality.

"So why are they still hunting Professor Wong? Why are you still stomping across worlds that seem empty, yet kill hundreds? Why do the MIA counts keep rising?"

I see his brows furrow. He'll either talk or engage.

His elbow flicks outward. We trained for weeks to get the 'nought to kill' time down to quicker than most people can react. The enhanced projectile comes from his open-ended holster at nearly twice the speed of sound. It stops eight millimetres from my face.

She does so love giving me a scare.

"Tiny death,
screaming ore,
fall to nature,
and exist no more."

The lilting refrain comes from the air to my left. The projectile turns to glowing dust and drifts away on the wind.

Tino staggers, eyes turning glassy. Bastard trick, overriding a man's own body.

"Mathrey, we need to be gone. They've puppeted him."

He vanishes. A tiny creature of midnight hues appears before me, hovering like a hummingbird on wings of molten silver.

"We knew they would. He was your friend. Their best chance to get close."

Sick betrayal ending a loyal career. Gods damn them all.

"Where did you flicker him to?"

She rests a tiny hand on my eyebrow.

"To the puppeteer's fortress in the sky."

That should get their attention. Nothing like your own human bomb arriving in your command centre to make you cautious.

Two squads of former Earth special forces appear about me, each member with one or more specialists from the Nineteen Realms as partners.

"Mathrey, let First Envoy Kresdall know that I waive my objections. The only way to stop this, and to save the Twentieth Realm, is to save the humans that infest it from themselves."

"That which Earther politicians call an 'intervention'?"

"No, Mathrey. We go with honesty, as always. This means war."

Harrowed

"Well, now. What do we have here?"

I yelp in surprise and shoot him. He disappears from view. There's a splash.

"Did he just fall into water?"

"Definitely sounded like something wet."

"Does that mean we've arrived somewhere useful?"

"No idea. Go look."

"You're the mad scientist who dragged his family into warp space using a faulty home-made hyperdrive."

She's got me there. I lift my tired bones off the bottom of the pool and peer over the edge.

"We're a barge. In a river. I see boats with flashing lights coming this way."

"Told you that gun was loud."

Dammit.

"Dad, our barge is leaking."

I look down. The turquoise ceramic of the tropical paradise pool has finished translating itself. It's now the hold of a derelict barge that clearly hasn't been maintained in a very long time. Still a long way from the garden shed it started out as.

"Looks like we're swimming."

"Dad, let's dive off the opposite side to the flashies. Shoot the hyperdrive as we go."

"Can't do that, Nancy, it's our way back!"

She slaps me.

"Your fucking way got us lost, got my stepmom and Max eaten by some alien monstrosity, then sent Jimmy running off with a Terbulantic dancer. There are no answers in your delusion. Use your busted machine again? Fuck no. We need to get off this ride somewhere liveable before something kills you and I end up dead – or doing something fucking awful to survive on a world I don't belong in."

"You swear too much."

"Apart from that: I'm fucking right, and I'm fucking leaving. Come if you want."

Nancy runs across the hold, scrambles up the far side and drops from view. There's another splash. Damn... Oh, balls to it. My daughter's clearly the brains of this outfit. I run across the hold, clamber up on the edge, then pause while I take aim at the flawed device that started all this. I shoot it twice, then drop the gun into the hold and roll off the side of the barge.

The explosions behind are accompanied by a lightshow that makes our short swim easier. I get to the ladder as Nancy reaches the top, and make it halfway up before the final blast flattens me against the embankment. Maintaining my hold with difficulty, I force myself to climb. After clawing my way over the edge, I make myself ignore the sirens and run with her.

She darts to the left. I hear a startled cry. Before I can gather myself to look, she's back.

"Got a bag. No, I didn't kill anyone. Hopefully there's money in it, and the thing sticking out is some sort of newspaper."

Who is this? Three years ago she screamed for a day after we had to scramble back to the transformed shed through a jungle filled with insects the size of cars. Two years ago she was hysterical over seeing her dog eaten, but still dragged me away from Anne's severed leg so we could escape. She was the one who bandaged the wound where Jimmy stopped my arguing with a long knife, hatred burning in his eyes.

"What now?"

We run a long way before she scoots down an alley and settles herself.

"Sit down. Time to turn your brilliant mind to being a criminal. I love you for trying to fix your fuck ups, hate you for not quitting sooner, haven't forgiven you for getting Max killed, and I'll leave you if I need to."

My daughter, the survivor. Hope I can keep up.

Girls' Night Out

It looks so normal: open woodland by the light of the moon. You couldn't tell it's laid with concealed barricades, barbed wire in the undergrowth, and pits of varying sizes all over the place. The spaces between the trees are webbed with razor wire or piano wire. They definitely don't want visitors.

Shame.

"G."

The command comes over my net, abbreviated to keep transmission times minimal. I use an IR link to let the girls know we're on, then brace myself. No matter how many times you practice, long-legs take a toll on your knees and ankles.

We go through the unfriendly woods at 30kph, being sensible about it, letting our sensors figure out what's where and what not to tread on: the landmines remain undisturbed.

Breaking from the treeline first, I take a snap bearing and use my jump jets to put me on the top of the nearest tower. An unlucky sentry provides a soft landing.

Straightening up, I watch the girls accelerate from the woods and run straight up the walls, tails straight back, not even bobbing with effort.

There's a scream. There's always a scream. I zoom in to see a terrified guard stabbing at Betty. She feints left, feints right, then rocks back on her tail and kicks him in the groin so hard it lobs him over the wall. She shoots me a toothy grin, then is gone towards the door at the end of the battlements.

Carla and Doris leap from the walls, legs coiled so they can kick out at the roof of the barracks just before they go through it. Over half the roof goes in, then body parts start coming out. I'll be shocked if any of the opposition make it to the door.

Where on earth is Edith?

A cone of flame curves across the courtyard. The flames reflect monochromatically in gleaming blue-black panels, pick highlights from the multi-faceted optics, and flash in the curved mirrors that are the talons of Sony-Yaskawa AIDino No. 4, known to her friends as Edith Killraptor. She jumps the fiery spray, lands, and whips her tail round to let the shockwhip that occupies the last metre hit the flamethrower trooper across the throat. His eyes actually light up! Cybergear short circuit: he's fried.

There's a crash, followed by a scream. Unusual. The screaming usually ends with a 'crash'. A body plummets in a shower of glass and lands head first. The screaming stops. Ah-ha. Across in the keep, through that smashed window, I see Betty confronting what must be a cybered-up officer. Their moves are fluid, and the woman blocks strikes without losing bits of herself.

Betty tries a pincer move to the neck and the woman grabs both her upper arms, flexing them down to prevent slashing attacks from hind legs. She grins. Betty opens her mouth like she's laughing too, then shoots the woman in the face using the 10mm pistol mounted in the roof of her mouth. Ouch. Officer down, medic not required.

In one corner of the courtyard, a figure in the remains of a familiar uniform hangs by one arm from a torture frame of some kind. His other hand waves placatingly as Edith slowly advances. Brave soldier.

Edith pops me a query: "KL?"

That's one of ours, so: "N."

"Trooper! Can you lead us to the rest of the captives?"

He looks up at me, then gestures haltingly toward a door to my left, signing for two right turns, then guards.

"EK, release the friendly."

She examines the frame for a moment, then kicks it to bits. The soldier gingerly unties his arm. That's at least a couple of dislocations he's nursing.

Carla and Doris bounce out of the barracks covered in blood.

"Trooper, you up for guiding us?"

He nods.

"Okay. You can talk to the girls and they'll understand. CK, DK, EK: go with."

He waves and leads the way.

There's still screaming coming from the keep. I know what that is.

"BK, stop playing with your prey. We're leaving."

I get an icon in reply: a raptor with its tongue out. The screaming gets frantic, then stops. She reappears on the battlements within thirty seconds.

Three minutes, five bursts of gunfire and one scream later, my three girls lope out and disappear over the walls. Betty follows them after checking on me. I wave her on.

Ten people follow the trooper out, looking about in wide-eyed amazement. I bounce down to the courtyard in two moves and check our foundlings over. Nothing too severe. I call in the airlift. My proximity alert tells me it's inbound almost immediately. Must have been loitering. Nice to know they were so confident in my girls.

I point to the soldier.

"These people are yours to marshal, trooper. We were never here."

He grins and nods.

"Yes, ma'am."

I take the stairs to the battlements four at a time, then hop over the wall and use my jump jets to land neatly.

"Killraptors! On me!"

The girls stride over and gather.

"Time to go. Stealth up and let's get a shift on."

All five of us become shrouded in holographic patterns of night and invisible countermeasures. We disappear down the road from the castle at a comfortable 45kph. The extraction flight passes overhead, transport oblivious to our presence, the gunship noticing but giving no sign except a burst: "JWD."

'Job well done'. Too right. We're becoming legends and rumours are the other side is scrambling to come up with something similar. Going to be an interesting battlefield when they arrive. Until then, we'll keep on scaring and saving by killing and disappearing.

Broken Wings

Slowly revolving like Christmas decorations, sparkling under the spotlights of the *Seacole*.

The barbarism of those we face brought an old quote back to me: 'An honest soldier will regard the battlefield as dawn breaks across it on the morn after the battle. He will take in the awful beauty revealed. Set against the death-dealing evidenced by that vista, something he knows full well, having oft dealt such, he must acknowledge the sacrifices made. He should then give thanks unto God for his survival, no matter it be by the fortunes of war or the vicissitudes of rank.'

Every time I come to a field like this, I start by looking at it unfiltered, admitting my relief at not being part of it.

"When you're ready, Jackie."

We call the enemy 'Triclaws'. Not much is known about them: secretive, ruthless, and never ones for what humanity considers a 'fair fight'. They're also arrogant and bloodthirsty: obviously in possession of technology good enough to baffle or evade our many forms of detection and surveillance, yet preferring to tear their victims to pieces instead of using ranged weaponry if given the slightest opportunity.

Merciless, overwhelming force is their trademark. We have some basic descriptions: at least two metres tall, two clawed arms on one side, a giant pincer on the other. There may be other limbs, because they can use our keyboards and the like. They never leave their dead, and delight in taunting us. In confirmation of their arrogance, every atrocity is capped with some disgusting trophy display. When it comes to space battles, they leave only wings and fins.

"Seacole, I'm going in."

We search every site. The first clue we got was from a lone tech on an isolated orbital station. She took one of them out. Had to use herself as bait, and kill herself, to manage it. Left us a description and some clues. Since then, re-investigations have revealed many supposed accidents as likely Triclaw attacks.

They aren't infallible. Horrifically good, hinting at long practice, but not perfect. Their advantage is in leaving so little of themselves behind. One fine day we'll bury them. Painstaking efforts like this are how it'll come to pass.

"What are you thinking, Jackie?"

"That we should change our parameters. The Triclaws obviously use heat sensors. I'd guess movement detection too. For anyone to survive a post-battle purge, they would need to be cold and still. Everybody knows, so anyone with the skills and materials would have to be fast."

"And lucky?"

"Only if we find them alive."

"True. We reckon whatever they came up with would be of diminishing effectiveness, too."

So, my theoretical survivor is hiding in plain sight – or inside plain sight.

"Seacole, give me a 3D map of the debris field. Highlight all remains with an internal volume over a square metre."

This search would be nonsensical if the Triclaws hadn't taken everything but the wings. My grid fills with coloured debris.

"How long since the battle, do we reckon?"

"Twenty hours."

"I'm heading towards the nearest. Scan the others for raised temperature. There's no way to hide body heat for that long without prepared containment."

Please. I want to prove they're not perfect killers.

"Jackie, the ventral fin from the 'HSS Expedient' is warm! A check of the original schematics reveals it had a manned weapons cubicle that was sealed up during a refit. It's flashing on your grid."

That's a way off.

"Seacole, I'll rendezvous there. Go get them."

Darkness returns as the *Seacole* moves off.

The thing that offends me most is how pretty the wreckage looks in the light of the distant sun.

I take my time and check all the other possibles. Finding two would be a miracle, but I have to be thorough.

"He's alive, Jackie."

Here's hoping he's got information: another rivet for the Triclaws coffin.

Vindictive

I wake with a dagger in my hand. The other end of the dagger is in someone's neck. Raising my gaze, I see the life fade from his eyes. The moment stretches as details sketch themselves in around the face of someone I don't know. A ship's bridge. Crew members staring in horror. A purple and green planet on the view screens.

The nearest person's gaze flicks to my left. Something hits me from the left. I'm knocked down, dagger seemingly locked in my hand. Blood fountains across my falling view. I hit the floor, then hit my head. Darkness.

"Is she awake?"

"She's coming round, sir."

I open my eyes. The ceiling is blue, the lighting soft and indirect.

"Welcome back, Shistal. If that's your real name."

It's not.

"Becky. Rebecca. Rebecca Ethelsdotter."

"Dotter? You're from the Scandic Worlds?"

"Issker."

"Why do you have greenish skin?"

I raise my hand. Long fingers. Their colour is wrong. I giggle.

"Eisa said I had green fingers. Don't think she meant it literally."

"Eisa?"

"My sister."

Him!

"*Faen!*"

"What's wrong?"

"Eisa got a new boyfriend. Madden Lars. I thought he was a creep, and that was before he tried it on. I told her, she finished with him. He said he'd get me for doing that."

"How is this pertinent?"

"She said he described his job as 'cyberpsychiatrist'. We laughed about robots lying on a couch. A few days later, I found out what they do is adjust behaviour with implants."

A bearded man with blue eyes leans into my view.

"We'll have to continue this conversation later. Something just came up."

It goes quiet, then crewmembers come in and wheel whatever I'm lying on into a grey room. I hear the door close with a hiss.

The bearded man reappears.

"Sorry about that. I think I got where you were going with that line of thought. Hold still. We're about to do a passive scan."

"Why passive?"

"Because I think anyone who set you up with an implanted cyber-identity so you could assassinate someone, but rigged it to have you live long enough to realise, is nasty enough to have booby-trapped it. That's why I moved you to a shielded room: so this Madden or whoever he works for can't detonate you before we're done."

Swallowing hurts; my mouth has gone dry.

He leaves. Time passes. Things hum and stop, then click and stop, then hum again. There's a hissing noise. Things get blurry. Darkness.

"Welcome back, Rebecca."

I'm lying in a bed with a raised back. The bearded man is sitting to one side. There's a nurse on the other. A uniformed man stands by the door.

"Was I booby-trapped?"

He nods.

"Very much so. You'd been set up to injure or kill everyone near you. The medical team have taken it all out. Our security team have already extracted enough information to prove that, despite your body being used, you're not actually guilty."

"What about Madden?"

"He's been arrested and taken off Issker for questioning. I also requested a protective detail for your family. Just in case."

"I thought he meant it, too. But I was preparing for petty vandalism, not kidnapping."

"It certainly raises some dark possibilities. You'll be questioned when you return home. They're sending a vessel to collect you. Until then, you get to enjoy the cruise from this private room in our medical centre."

"Thank you."

Questioning isn't the problem. I'm more concerned about how I stop being green.

Finding the Truth

The roof is a tarpaulin, sheltering walls braced with lengths of burnt wood and fungus-like runs of building foam. The floor had been churned mud before a levelling blazer converted it to blackened glass. At the centre of the room a figure is tied to a chair, clothing reduced to rags. Wires criss-cross his body. Everything's covered in dirt, except for the officer leaning on the wall in front of the figure. She's gazing at a holographic display that floats in the air between them.

"Let's try again, Captain Thirm. You claim your unit intercepted Major Proth's retreat. Somehow, despite managing to kill all the grunts, you missed him."

The figure in the chair spits.

"Interrogator Reed, my reply stands: your commander is a prick."

The veracity indicator flashes bright green.

"Still telling the truth." She coughs. "From his point of view."

The shadowed image in the video window wobbles as a fist slams into the camera.

"I told you to stop him doing that!"

"Commander, the only way to do that will render him unable to reply."

A face looms close enough for the light from the screen to pick out the shine of his scars.

"I authorise the use of special measures."

"Commander, we've been making this man's nervous system light up like a Christmas tree for three days. In that time, the only information we've obtained is 1,442 reiterations of his opinion of you. The time for psionic interrogation is when the subject's neurosurgical landscape is uncompromised, where the nuances between truth, lie, and obfuscation can be discerned."

"I emphasised special measures. Turning him into a vegetable is acceptable."

"Commander, use of that discipline is an atrocity under the Convention of Mars. I refuse."

"If you disobey me, mindwarper, I'll have you shot for treason."

There's a pause, then she steps through the holographic display and places her hand on the Captain's head. His body jerks. On screen, the shadowed figure nods.

Thirm finds himself unable to move. A burning sensation races about in his head, becomes almost unbearable, then vanishes. A voice speaks within his mind.

Hello, Walter. I see you volunteered for experimental pain buffering. It seems to have worked. I've also browsed other relevant memories. I see events occurred as you reported, and can detect no interference. Do you have any idea why the official record disagrees with the truth you participated in?

Walter struggles for a moment, then works out how to reply.

We overran this sector far quicker than expected. Proth had to improvise, starting with the decoys my team met. The Commander has fresh scars. From ten years ago? I patched him up after that battle. Also, like most of our side, he has no problem with psionicists. Commander Adams would never use a derogatory term like 'mindwarper'.

You're insinuating that the Major has hidden himself within our chain of command?

Remote warfare has unique hazards. Proth seems to have exploited them. He's getting the witnesses killed during interrogations. Tell whoever's going in to be careful. He'll be guarded by the survivors of his Special Tactics Executive.

Excuse me.

He's alone in his head, her hand still in place. Minutes pass.

The shadowy figure on screen slumps sideways and disappears. A woman in PsiCom uniform takes his place.

"Initial reads confirm the hypothesis. We have captured Major Proth and one STE operative."

Her hand lifts from his head.

"Welcome back, Captain. You're reinstated, and are scheduled to return to duty after a ten-day furlough."

"Join me for a drink?"

"I've been in your mind."

"I'll take that as a 'no'."

Requiescat

Space, the never-ending frontier, the long night, the sea of stars. That last one should have given us a warning. Look what we did to the seas of Earth: filled them with our discards to the point where we nearly choked the planet.

"Ping ping ping, Reiter."

"Three hits?"

"Close formation, no movement."

"Leftovers."

Saldi hums the first few bars of a death rite from Chal-Dy-Mer, her homeworld.

"What are the words that go with that?"

She pauses for a moment, lips moving as she translates.

"It loses a lot, along with the rhyme and meter, but put roughly, it's 'let them who scavenge from graves, be taken in their stead, that the number of evil hearts be reduced, and life be better for it.'"

"I could get behind the idea. Shall we?"

She nods.

We switch to manoeuvring thrusters and sidle up to the trio. A quick look confirms our suspicions: these freespace burials have been looted. The coffins have been stripped of panels; corpses broken in the haste to remove anything that might be of value.

"Stripship?"

That would be my guess, too.

"Agreed. Two-suit team on umbilicals cracked them open. One tore the coffins apart, the other smashed through the bodies. I'd guess they chucked it all into a haulage sack and got wound back in. Done and gone really fast."

"No point in looking for identification. I'll get samples for the Book."

The Great Book of Remembrance: a huge database containing DNA samples from every cadaver found drifting, along with any names or identifying marks remaining.

We've been blundering around out here for nearly five hundred years. Our dead have been recognised navigational hazards for the last three hundred. The sheer arrogance of casually punting corpses into space caught our neighbours, the Cheteny and the Klact, by surprise. Took them a while to work out a currently spacefaring race was being so inconsiderate. When they found out we also let our lost ships stay lost, they pointedly enquired if we were going to pay them to clean up after us.

Starside Recovery Division was created soon after that. Spacers can call us to come and deal with any debris they come across. We'll either handle it directly or refer it to the owning race. Our clearing up is done with as much reverence as we can spare, and always guarantees the sanctity of any cadaver enclosures and their contents.

Strippers make a living by scavenging from the dead. Stripships turn that ghoulish activity into a business in relics and scrap. Frequently, a stripship will support their own crew as well as acting as a hub for a mob of independent strippers.

"Where's the nearest sun?"

I check the navigational archives.

"A month at sublight. We'll need to burn them."

Our preferred way to let cadavers go is to send them into a star. I like to think that fits with the intent of the original burials. However, when doing so would mean sending what amounts to an unmonitored missile on a long journey, we use ship armaments to vaporise the remains instead.

"Sad but true. I'll back us off. You ready the beamers."

Saldi leaves us slowly drifting away from the sombre cluster. I bring the dorsal battery to bear and task the starboard side anti-meteor quadmounts with catching any scatter.

She and I chorus the **SRD** saining for the dead.

"Now we lay thy bodies down, that thine souls may find surcease should it have been denied them. *Requiescat in pace.*"

Blinding energy beams make the remains coruscate, then disintegrate. The long night resumes.

Observers

The dimly-lit long hall is made darker by burning incense and the herbs being smoked by every non-human present except for me. It's my first time as an 'Impartial Witness' with humans involved; my familiarity with the Rugoshin is why I'm here.

Sitting opposite the human delegation from Hassanad are the leaders of the Kloctanggy Preeminence, the greatest of the Eminences that rule the four habitable planets of the Rugosh I and III systems. Green exoskeletons shine as quadruple pupils – three vertical on the left, a single larger on the right, above a fanged mouth – narrow in disgust.

I know the Rugoshin well. They're fierce, loyal, and make fantastic stews. They're fearless fighters, have three physical sexes, multiple genders, and non-Rugoshin can't tell them apart. Even with my experience, I still have trouble distinguishing *clettl* from *clettr* without seeing them move. *Clettn* I can spot from speech patterns. As for gender, I never guess: I ask should it become relevant.

"Why do you demand *trishmash* service?"

Bargny is the highest rank here. *Clettr* is an *Obandurk*: approximately equivalent to a mythological Terran demigod made manifest, as far as I can make out.

Vice President Mark Parkes starts to raises a placating hand, then stops when his interpreter informs him that the gesture will be regarded as contemptuous.

'*Trishmash*' carries connotations of obligation and exclusivity. I'm curious how he'll pitch the reply.

"We're simply seeking you as an ally against the forces of Nemble. With your cohorts fighting alongside our armoured divisions, we will be assured of victory."

I see nods. 'Victory' is an almost universally understood concept. Nobody engages in war seeking defeat, after all.

"You should slay your *Kldurk*. At least, force a *Durkitra*. They are *mesham*."

Looks of confusion are exchanged on the human side of the table.

Not surprising. Bargny just suggested the Hassanad should replace their parliament, either by outright murder or by having each of them fight up to three challengers to keep their positions. The reason being that they're all cowards and weaklings. Parkes is a member of that parliament. I hope his interpreter spots the need to reply forcefully to the tacit insult.

I see him wave the interpreter's suggestion aside, ignoring the fact gestures like that have been highlighted as unwise. The Rugoshin exchange glances and clickspeak. Antenna crests rise.

"Why on Earth would we do that? I am perfectly capable. I myself served in the army for two years before entering parliament."

Bargny waves in an exact copy of the vice president's gesture to the interpreter. Parkes squawks, then his head collapses in a spurt of dark fluid. An odour of cooked meat fills the room. The Rugoshin guard keep their weapons levelled at the human delegation until Bargny and his colleagues have departed, then follow them out.

The Hassanad delegation departs quickly, leaving only a handful of staff to attend to both logistics and body. After a short while, all bar one have found excuses to be elsewhere. Only Parliamentary Deputy Peter Trellis is left, still heaping tissues to soak up the mess before it ruins more of the discarded documents on the table. Watching him carefully, I understand: he's not trying to save the documents, he's trying to stop it running onto the floor.

Seeing my attention is on him, he beckons me over.

"Witness Khren, what just happened?"

I check my protocols. There is nothing left for me to risk influencing. The negotiations have concluded.

"The Rugoshin attended today out of curiosity. They have had reports from the various mercenaries and adventurers of their race that have ventured outside the Rugosh systems. They are a combative race, but they no longer engage in mass warfare, considering it barbaric. Disputes are settled by single combat, be they quarrels between families or disagreements between nations: Rugoshin of equivalent standing face off, one per faction, and fight until only one remains uncontested. The views of the victor become the truth or the new way.

"It is puzzling to see hundreds of them gather upon a battlefield, then set up camps while individuals meet and contest to prove their mettle, standing, or fitness to form a family or join an Eminence. Away from those contests, friends and families from different Eminences meet, catch up, and share meals.

"But I digress. To employ someone from outside the disputing parties to fight on one's behalf is forbidden. Mercenaries were unknown to the Rugoshin until humanity discovered their superb martial skills. It is permitted because it allows the Rugoshin to gather information about humanity and the other races out here."

Peter looks over his notes, then stares at me. I presume his expression should communicate something, but I'm not familiar enough with humans.

"Would I be right in guessing the Rugoshin consider humans to be barbaric? Specifically, they hold our methods of warfare in contempt?"

"You are correct in both."

He looks relieved.

"This also explains the absolute refusal of Rugoshin mercenaries to fight against other Rugoshin."

"Correct."

He smiles! I am perplexed.

"Please explain your levity. It does not fit with my understanding of the failure I have just witnessed."

Peter uses a sterile wipe to clean his hands, throws it on the pile, then steps away from the table.

"I'd be happy to explain. You're an 'Impartial Witness', I'm a 'Covert Observer'. I suspect we have similar roles, with the main difference being that in addition to your observation and reporting, you can be called upon to referee, whereas I covertly observe under the guise of a junior functionary, and then report to United Worlds."

"A duty in some way similar to the implicit duty of Rugoshin mercenaries."

He smiles.

"Vaguely. Anyway, what happened today was something my superiors had been hoping would happen. The prospect of organised Rugoshin forces entering an alliance with any human faction caused my superiors a great deal of worry. To know they will never do that, plus the additional reassurance of knowing they will never ally with another race, is remarkably comforting."

It seems there are depths to some of these humans we should be wary of.

I smile, then close my mouth as he pales. I'm told we Zhallyx have 'too many teeth' for humans to remain comfortable when we do that.

"Thank you, Peter. I wish you good fortune on your travels."

"And to you, Witness Khren," he pauses, "that's not your name, is it?"

"Just as yours isn't Parliamentary Deputy Peter Trellis."

I smile and take my leave.

Dirty Badge

"Hey, Cherry. Who's that freak you know? Reynard?"

Constable Dalforth grins nastily.

Inspector Cherry Fasslin of the Tactical Response Group grimaces. He knows she knows exactly who he's insulting. She also knows he wouldn't say word one if that particular gent were actually nearby.

"It's Reinhardt. Why?"

"Maybe you should call him. The polar bear has a katana. Might be a challenge."

Cherry sighs. She's spent so long working on animorph relations with members of the regular police. This caveman seems to have missed every session.

"Constable Dalforth, that's a white-pelted ursimorph with an *ōdachi*. Calling it a polar bear might offend it, and calling it's heirloom monumental blade a small sword is sure to."

"I see a furball with a samurai sword, I'm not worried about the niceties. I call in the TRG. You are the TRG, aren't you?"

Officer Lupin Blue has moved up on Dalforth's blind side.

"Boo."

Her whispered greeting causes him to jump, literally, which ruins his trained response to spin, crouch, and be ready to defend or draw. He lands with his feet mid-move and stumbles sideways until he bounces off a gyrocar.

"'kin' 'ell, a moggie." His voice is flat with anger.

Cherry winces. Definitely missed every session.

Lupin's ears drop flat.

"That would be felimorph, but you're forgiven. Once."

"'kin' TRG..."

His red-faced reply trails off as the barking laughter of the ursimorph gets louder.

Cherry looks over. It's leaning on a lamppost, ōdachi resting on a shoulder, pointing at Dalforth.

"You can't dance for shit, notepad."

Dalforth's hand goes to his sidearm.

"What did he just call me?"

Officer Joe Tremaine, the other member of Cherry's patrol, places a hand on the shoulder of Dalforth's gun arm.

"He called you a 'Notepad'. It's military slang for a police officer who's not as tough as they act. I think he's nailed you, mate."

Dalforth glances about.

Cherry hopes he sees what she does: Joe is leaning forward, using his long reach, so he has room to react. Lupin's taken two steps back, and has a hand on her sidearm. If Dalforth tries anything, he'll be down before his piece clears the holster.

The laughter stops.

"Ey, TRG boss lady. You the one who knows our Cat?"

Cherry gives a quick smile and discreetly gestures for the snipers to stand down.

"Had dinner at her and Marie's place last night. What's with the blade, big bear? Bit late in the day for a shave."

The ursimorph chuckles, swings a giant scabbard round from behind, then sweeps the ōdachi into it with a single, smooth movement. Standing with the scabbarded blade in one hand, it salutes her.

"I'm Captain Seiji Guevara. Been away for a while. Got myself turned about in these rebuilt back ways, saw a uniform exchanging packets with someone, went to ask directions. The someone scarpered. The uniform screamed and drew on me. I had a flashback, caught it in time, but drew before I stepped back. We were in a standoff until he holstered his piece when you lot rolled in."

Cherry nods. As it happens, she recognises his name. Reinhardt mentioned it last night.

"Officer Blue, could you update Captain Guevara's datapad with the latest Southwark maps? Then we'll let him get on his way."

She checks her datapad, then glares at Dalforth.

"After that, we're going to have a long chat with Constable Dalforth about why he's so far from his beat, who that someone was, what's in the other packet, and why he's so jumpy."

Dalforth swallows so hard they hear it.

Joe chuckles: "Gotcha, dirty badge."

Why Did You Run?

I've been a fool for many things, but she who survived the cyber-conversion with me has always been my only weakness. That was true even before we fought and bled alongside each other for six years. At first, we kept a distance. When we both got our own squads, the need for restraint went too. We quickly came to sharing quarters.

You were always the pragmatic one. I was too much of an optimist, even in the midst of a war that saw planets stripped of their atmospheres, and entire armies sacrificed. We swore we'd survive, swore we'd stay loyal - to each other, at least.

Then came Mohgren, and the infamous order to retreat. On the surface, all we knew was that every line to Command went dead. They left us to fight and die. Unbeknownst to all bar Command, the retreat was sector-wide. The Danshe had managed to get portal ships into place at Lagrange points in eleven systems. Their reinforcements were pouring through in numbers we couldn't hope to defeat.

"Seven years, Cass. I spent seven years crawling around on Mohgren, more swamp creature than soldier."

I see a tear start from the corner of an eye.

"For five years after that, I worked my way across human-held space. I tracked down every ship that didn't make it to the fleet rendezvous at Latullus. Every. Single. One. You weren't rostered on any of them. None of your squad were."

You nod.

"Two years ago, an old skipper told me he'd seen a Peryton cloak up in the Mohgren system before the fleet withdrew. There were no orders to cloak. Orders were to save power for retreat manoeuvres. Took me a year to find that Peryton. Still had Scalzy in command. He looked like he'd seen a ghost when I sat down opposite him. Then he told me this crazy story about you getting all het up when the retreat order came. Said you lost it completely, talked the whole squad into deserting. Saved their lives by doing so, because we all know what happened to the fleet after it gathered in the Latullus system."

You wave for me to sit. Unconsciously graceful as ever.

"He said you just lit out on your own at the first port they hit, never even said goodbye. Nobody had a clue where you went. Took me a while, but I remembered what you'd said about your childhood."

You tilt your head and smile.

"Madagascar."

Your voice is hoarser, but still the one I fell for when I first heard it over comms.

"Took me a while to get here, and I'll not interrupt your new life for long. I just want you to tell me one thing: why?"

I'm waiting for a flood. Of tears, or apologies, maybe both. But there's no guilt in your eyes. Instead, you hold out a hand, and not towards me.

She comes into the room, lean and barefoot, wearing your old off-duty bodysuit, sleeves rolled up, her wiry hair tied back. I see the circuitry that webs her arms and face, the sensors in the fingertips she extends to you. There's a smudge of dirt on her button nose. When she turns to look at me, I see the smudge extends along her cheekbone. I recognise it. I get the same when I try to rub my nose while I'm work-

Her eyes are mine. It's like looking into the eyes of a younger me.

"Sarah, this is your dad."

There's no hesitation. She lunges and wraps her arms about me.

"Mum said you'd find us!"

I extend a hand to Cass. No more explanations.

The Peace of Fireflies

I used to watch the fireflies, seeing how they flitted and settled. They seemed to go everywhere, but never intruded on the air above the still waters of the mere. Just like the fireflies above that mere never strayed anywhere else.

As time went by, I noticed the fireflies of the mere were unusual in other ways: appearing all year round being the main thing. I also came to the strange certainty that there were a fixed number of them. But I found a peace like nowhere else, sitting on the shore of the mere and watching those fireflies gather near me.

Before I could follow up on the strangeness, the onset of puberty and life in general distracted me. Thus it was many years before a breakup led to a trip home and an evening of melancholy. As heartache often does, it sought nostalgia to dwell upon: my memories of the fireflies.

Which is why I found myself sitting on the shore of the mere tonight, watching as the fireflies came closer.

They seem quicker. Eager, even. But the peace is still here.

"Bertha."

I lurch to my feet, spinning to put my back to the water. I'd prefer a wall, but this will have to do. The eerie light of my flying companions shows me very little, until he moves.

"Dunc. What are you doing here?"

I know, but I need him to acknowledge it, or confirm my worst fears – or both.

"You never brought me here. You talked about it, but never invited me. So I invited myself. You know, to be with you. To be us, in your special place."

He comes closer.

Both, then.

"Dunc, we're over. It wasn't working."

"For you! Not for me!"

He's got a knife! Too far to anywhere useful from here. That's part of its appeal. This isn't good.

"What's with the knife, Dunc?" Keep the tone casual.

He looks at it. Then looks at me, at the mere, and smiles.

"Thought we could go together, you know? Show them we had something special."

His other hand dives into a pocket, emerging with a crumpled envelope.

"Did us a letter. So they'll know. They'll all know, those sad fucks who said I was bad for you. They'll know and be sorry they didn't have what we had."

His obsessive streak appealed to me at the start. Big mistake. How do I...?

"Dunc, let's go get a drink. We can talk about things."

"No! The time for talking is over. You said that."

I did.

"So it's time for action."

The knife comes up as he steps towards me. I back into the mere. Maybe it's got a drop-off: I'll disappear before he gets me.

I'm still backing up. He's in the water too. It's only up to my knees.

"Help." It's whisper, but it's the best I can do.

Fireflies dive into the water. A glow spreads between me and Dunc, getting stronger with each one that hits. He wades straight into the glowing patch, then stops.

He drops the knife. Reaches for me. It's not hostile. It's pleading. His eyes start to glow. He topples into the luminous water and sinks from view.

The fireflies come out of the water. They're brighter. One hovers right in front of me. A gem-like body, shining wings that don't move, and eyes like orbs of mercury.

A reedy voice. Hissing, crackling.

"Never come into the water alone. We'd have no choice."

I sprint from the place, screaming my thanks.

It'll still be peaceful.

But never for me.

Not now.

"It is a Land of Poverty..."

Midnight, the witching hour. I could do with a flying broom, come to think of it. On that topic, I suspect I've more chance of getting to know a broom than any witch that might flit about on one. Right, all geared up - or am I?

Phone, keys, medical cards, proof of being me, both permits to carry, handset, mask... No, wait. The evening DAQI was 11, with warnings about it hitting teens before dawn because of smog blowing in from the burning portions of Europe. Best go with the respirator and tuck the mask into the rucksack along with the thermos and food.

Check tonight's route while riding down to the car park. Oh joy: Bognor. At least I left my box of nitrile gloves in the rucksack. I can double glove before gauntlets without paying company rates for extras. The phone chirps. Good timing! Delly's outside. Saves me pollution charges from the commute.

Out through the triple doors into the cold.

It fills my view: cross a refuse wagon with a windowless coach, paint it brown, add twin fat black stripes round the cab. The modern dead-cart. No need to bring them out, we'll take them from where they fell.

I swing up into the changing room and shout through the open door to the cab.

"What you doing bringing the company limo out to fetch staff?"

Delly laughs.

"In case you missed it, your place is on a B-optimal route to Bognor. As there are pile-ups or roadworks on the A-optimals, I thought I'd show due diligence, and do you a favour."

"It's brass primate castration season out there. Tonight could be a bad one."

"You need to use bigger words in your fancy slang. I can still make out what you mean."

"And your sarcasm needs work. I'm not bleeding. So, tonight?"

She nods.

"You're not wrong. We've got three police call-outs already. Good news is those gave me priority for Arnie."

I swing open the door to the cadaver processor - which I can only do because it's not in use yet - and grin at the bulky, four-armed robot.

"Hello, Arnie."

The bucket-shaped head turns my way. Lenses whine as it focusses on me. Takes a few moments for facial recognition, then it waves.

"Hello, Poppy. Are we playing chess tonight?"

"Don't think so, Arnie. It looks busy."

"I like to be busy."

"See you later."

I close the door and it goes back to doing whatever it does when no-one is looking.

We take the old road to Bognor. As we traverse the long, curved bridge just before we hit the outskirts, I see blue lights ahead.

An officer flags us down.

"You lot on duty?"

Delly nods.

"Cart 68, constable. What you got for us?"

The officer gestures towards the roof of a car just visible in the cutting.

"Whole family. I'd say the car holds everything they owned."

Delly looks at me. I glance back towards cadaver processing.

"Thank the gods for Arnie. Never thought we'd start the night with another Universal Credit failure."

She shrugs.

"A lot of these coastal towns never picked up after the depression of '22, and Universal Credit always causes financial problems. This month's been the first really cold one. Guess they decided to go as a family rather than wait for winter to take them piecemeal."

I press the 'Retrieval' button. Arnie deploys. We're all pretending to be blasé until a teddy bear falls from the smallest body as it's carried in.

Delly chokes out: "Early break?"

I wipe my eyes.

"Yeah. Somewhere bright."

Ghostsong

The crowd is getting bigger by the minute. If someone doesn't call in an Alien Liaison Agent, things could get ug-

"You the ALA?"

Marvellous. One of the overseers of crowd control had the brains to leave an officer on the outside waiting for me.

"Yes. Alien Liaison Agent Thandee Grace."

He leads me through the crowd. It's not as big as I thought. There's a lot of space inside the ring of people. Checking to either side, it's not just a lot of space: everybody is within leaping distance of some form of cover. What off Earth?

"I see the crowd. Where's the alien you need me to liaise with?"

The officer points.

"Far side of the fountain. I'd come with you, but can't leave my post."

I don't believe that, but I do sympathise with his urge to avoid danger.

Nothing to do but stroll across Centenary Park like it's a normal afternoon. Clear pink sky, blue clouds, violet sun, the tinkling hiss of minute crystals spraying from the nozzles of the fountain.

I see the blood before I round the corner. Pools of it. Sprays and spatters too. Someone's had quite the picnic.

Taking a deep breath, I round the corner with as much nonchalance as I can summon. As I dreaded, the blood trails lead to their sources – all dumped in an untidy pile at the hooves of the creature that sits on the plinth that surrounds the fountain.

Orange blotches pattern yellow skin, shading to yellow across grey hooves. Getting closer, I see smears of white across ground and skin. Huge hands are blue. They move constantly, prehensile fingers flicking like collections of paintbrushes across the white-painted face. The striping they leave is complex and strange.

Four of the five eyestalks atop the head turn my way.

"Liaisor Thandee. Come closer. There is no death remaining in me."

Chexn Krea doesn't stop painting its head as I move to stand by its side, counting bodies as I go.

"When did the Sage of the Pron'Tohr become a killer of eighteen?"

"That body found in the municipal tip? It was left behind by the ghost of Lixn Krea."

Victim of a racist attack, hunted like an animal through the storm drains before being gunned down. Damn and blast. Blinking back the start of tears, I gesture to the pile of corpses.

"These are those responsible?"

"And their firstborn. Apt, as they took mine."

A race so advanced, yet so primitive in their dealings regarding death and debt. Speaking of which, I have to ask.

"Does that not mean you have to forfeit your life?"

"Not so. I only took those who stood beside their parent in seeking to avert my retribution."

Then why is it painting itself?

"That's not a vengeance or death striping. If it's not sacrificial, it's something unknown to me. Is it another ritual striping I should learn?"

"No. It means nothing more than my ghost hurts and does not have anywhere else to put the pain."

I place a hand on its thigh, jump up using the ridge of a hoof, and plant myself next to it on the plinth, legs dangling. Taking a handful of spilled white, I plaster my face.

"Pass me some blue, Sage of the Pron'Tohr. Lixn Krea was a friend to me."

It hands me a pot of pigment, then points to the pile of bodies.

"What of them?"

I examine the blue trickling down my fingers.

"They and their ghosts will keep, Chexn Krea, along with all the bureaucracy. The only true thing left undone is taking a moment to honour our departed ghost."

It nods.

We sit and paint our faces as the sun goes down.

Page 314

"The Atrox is a perfect blend of artificially grown organics and 3D-printed cerametal. Able to withstand impacts that would crush a man to pulp, regardless of whether he is in body armour or not."

General Navores looks back down into the glass tank.

"It's very small, Cedric."

Inside, a strange feline form displays greenish-white flesh between strips of a blue crystalline substance. It moves fast, changing direction like a startled fly. Tiny claws and needle-like teeth flash as it snaps and slashes at the air.

"That's the beauty of it, sir. Fantastic infiltration capabilities, low noise, the option to use it for scouting ahead of primary mission groups as well as in active combat roles. Its resilience allows it to be delivered by unorthodox methods, such as hollow shells or missiles, in addition to drones."

The General sighs. This is the problem with boffins. So invested in their creations they become blind to any realities that might limit the applicability of their work to the real world.

"Cedric, I see the scouting potential, especially with that glorious video output."

He gestures towards the three-by-three 4K widescreen array on the far wall, showing him the little monster's less than flattering view of himself, its creator, and everyone else in the room: all thermal blurs and targeting icons.

"But active combat? Have you created a mouse-sized soldier to carry a sawn-off .22 while riding in a tiny saddle?"

His staff chuckle.

Cedric frowns. He stops watching his creation trying to kill invisible opponents, then points to the fat volume on the table between the General and his staff.

"Page 314."

The General looks at him.

"Pardon?"

"You haven't read as far as page 314."

The General directs a glare at his staff. They respond with a selection of gestures intended to convey 'we read the summary' and 'we were waiting for a digital copy'.

He turns back.

"What did I miss on that page, Cedric?"

"Readiness considerations."

The General grins.

"Like needing the opponents to be lying down?"

Cedric chuckles, then fixes the General with a withering stare.

"No, they can pyramid up a soldier faster than that soldier can reload. What I'm referring to is the figure at the foot the page: I have a million Atrox ready to deploy."

The General's eyes go wide. He watches the little terror move like nothing he's ever seen before, and lets his initial feeling of discomfort bleed through and blossom.

These things are going to revolutionise warfare - or end it.

New Record

The valley is smoking, trees nothing but scorched gravestones for the life they once sheltered. The farmland around here used to be really scenic, but the only tourists today are the subject of my little excursion.

"Good morning, Elizabeth. Welcome to this ashen paradise."

With Cardy as my control, this is going to be nothing but fun.

"Morning. Who am I partying with?"

"Seventeen hardcases with a penchant for scorched earth tactics."

They're good at their jobs. Holy hell, what a mess.

"Does anyone need to talk to them?"

"No."

"Do I need to be discreet?"

"No."

"Anything left I shouldn't hurt?"

"Don't be silly. Your targets just finished a sweep. They sure as shit ended anything living."

Then it's open season.

"Set the clock."

"Engage in 3... 2... 1... Go!"

I reverse the direction of my knees and charge, letting my targeting arrays prioritise victims by proximity as I accelerate to a whisker under 55KPH; I can't hit shit at anything over 60.

"They've spotted you."

"I'm leaving a rooster tail 10 metres high. You'd be wasting my time if they hadn't."

Powering up a low hill, I launch myself into a somersault, letting me shoot the three twats huddling in the lee before I land. Two down, one staggering.

"Left a stray."

"I've rolled a posse from 42 Commando in on your tail. Nothing's escaping."

The landing isn't as pretty as I'd like, but no-one's watching bar the boys and girls who've made me and my kind legendary, so I'm allowed a skid or two.

The next fire team is five strong with heavy weapons. I don't like GPMG. They scratch my plating. Plus, a close-range hit could tear my head off, but that's beside the point. A trio of minimissiles with frag heads leaves only their outlier.

He feints right, goes left, then breaks his dagger on the cerametal chainmail across my gut. Funny how ancient warfare tech often works really well when made with modern materials. I box his ears with my stubby assault rifles. He's wearing a helmet, but it doesn't matter. With titanium-wrapped weighted jackets on each barrel, I halve the width of his head.

The next mob are in two pairs, and enhanced. I can see their raised body temps. Which makes the colder sections revealing their junction boxes really easy to target with the baby railguns on my right arm. I only get ten titanium-coated ball bearings to play with, but they travel at four kilometres a second.

Three targets go down, crippled at best. The fourth is fastest, but a futile dodge only changes where he gets hit. Paired supersonic projectiles make a godawful mess of his head.

Last are the command team. Four around one. I go straight at them, flat out, assault rifles spitting. One goes down on the way in, the railguns do for his partner, and I'm on their leader before the furthest two can cover. She lets me have both barrels from a sawn-off shotgun, which hurts, and slows me down a bit. I'm going to be picking pellets out of my softer bits for a week.

Even slowed down, I still hit her at **45KPH** and stop dead, launching my empty guns into the last two. The transferred energy hurls her broken body away as the rifles knock her cohorts down. I pull my automatics. Simultaneous headshots finish the party.

Cardy whoops.

"**26** seconds from first contact. New record!"

Mission complete. I switch my knees back and retract the lenses over my eyes. I prefer to look passably human when I'm not being devastating.

Mind Your Step

The streetlights have been off for an hour. The rain has been constant for three. Through the sodden darkness comes a stranger, clad in earthy hues and righteousness.

I listen to him coming in. A mind is usually a noisy place, except in rare cases, or due to rigorous training. I'd say this intruder benefitted from both. He's actually playing back the briefing in his head while his body moves with thoughtless, flawless stealth.

"You'll be inserted just after full dark, with a window of sixty to ninety minutes. We know the target's active security stands down from nightfall to dawn. The reasons for that are still unclear, but we believe some form of automated system takes over during that time."

Fair guess, but wrong.

"Your suit gives you the profile of a small predator, so providing you don't move like anything else, even layered motion detectors will be nullified. We're sure there isn't any form of pressure grid or similar, as overflights have revealed no expanses of metal big enough."

Overflights? I'll pass that titbit to sky-side security. They'll be annoyed.

"Once inside the building, our intel indicates it was an average six-bedroom residence."

'Average'. Not a word I'd use for any home with six bedrooms.

"How it has been modified since is anyone's guess, but given our inability to strike the target - or even come close - we have to presume baffled corridors, airlocks, maze rooms, and likely a number of lethal-effect traps as well."

Walking through their secure sites unharmed must be a challenge.

Elsie interrupts my eavesdropping with a telepathic comment.

He's good. I didn't hear him open the door.

Yes. Definitely the best so far. Anton?

I don't recognise his intrinsic pathways. I'll need to dive him to get the details.

Which lets Elsie and I off the hook for tonight.

Is he far enough in to not hear the door relock?

Anton gets in before I instruct Elsie to hold off on using her telekinesis.

Better if he isn't. A trained mind like his will be momentarily unbalanced by the unexpected event.

Good enough.

Lock the door, Elsie. All yours, Anton.

The briefing playback stops dead as he hears the door lock behind him. I'll give him credit, he's an elite-plus operative. He immediately checks his vicinity, then starts running scenarios – interesting that they too are in briefing-playback style.

Then Anton barges into his mind. I see the kaleidoscopic explosion of interrupted consciousness, then get out before the insanity starts.

The best way to identify attackers is how they attack. Well, according to Anton, that is. I'm betting that without being able to map the 'shortcuts' the brain develops during training, it's an imprecise visual art. Problem with getting that deep into a mind is that the psychological damage from having someone else inside your head is ruinous.

I gently rouse one of the security detail.

Sorry, Randy, but there's a downed intruder in corridor three needing mercy.

He wakes fully, rises and heads out, grabbing one of the silenced pistols racked above the door to the ready room.

Anton calls us.

I had to keep him down until Randy shot him! Mental resilience like I've never encountered. He was ex-Delta recruited to a joint Lekem/GCHQ blacker-than-black outfit.

Who are Lekem?

Supposedly disbanded Israeli secret technology acquisition group.

That's grim but essential knowledge.

Elsie chips in.

She's undisturbed.

Using psionics openly attracts all the wrong kinds of attention. We'd been hiding for years. Then she quietly recruited us into the clandestine psionic outfit that protects her inner cadre.

We've not failed her yet.

VacSinHate

Opening clip: a heavily-built man sits on the tailgate of a blue pickup truck. He's smiling and unshaven, taking tiny sips from a red and white can of beer so quickly it doesn't interrupt his speech.

"Well, it's been difficult, that's for sure. Never thought them libtards could fight worth a damn, but Lord, they proved us all wrong about that. Digging them out of the sanctuary cities hereabouts took weeks. Can't say I held with the burnings and suchlike, but I do hold with our founders' proclamation that we have to be forthright in heart and deed, even if a few of those deeds sit badly with some folk's interpretation of the Good Book."

A band starts playing somewhere beyond his truck. He glances back, then his attention returns.

"We're not monsters or fanatics. The Free States of America are about individual rights and freedoms under the auspices of God. Can't say or be fairer than that."

Next clip: a thin woman leans against the wide shoulders of a bearded black man in a torn T-shirt. She starts, then the sentences go back and forth between them.

"After our warnings were ignored,"

"we discussed online,"

"before the nets went down,"

"and decided to become the haven for those who wanted to evade the lies,"

"the surveillance,"

"and the manipulation."

"Nobody tells us who lives,

"who dies,"

"what goes into our bodies,"

"or our minds."

They smile.

"We're part of the Independent States of America."

"If you want a chance to live free of the enslaved dystopia the rest of the world has fallen into,"

"come fight alongside us."

Followed by: an elderly woman gestures to the trees about them.

"When my son married a Lakota woman, we fought. Then he challenged me. I went to their reservation to prove him wrong. Instead I had an epiphany: realised what I was lacking. Never had much time for technology as it was presented, liked how it was used even less. Didn't take long to find out a lot of folk felt the same way.

"When things started to unravel, we gathered ourselves, chose our ground, and stood for what the spirits wanted. If you hear the call of the wolf, the eagle, or the crow, come find the Tribal Nations of America. Fight with us to save the land."

Then: a middle-aged man straightens his tie before pointing at the camera, his expression stern.

"You've got to understand that in trying to drain the swamp, he made himself a target. That he's still with us is a sign. The Evangelical States of America will be his legacy. The corporations he permits to trade here are all certified by the

Robertson Committee to be abiding by the Lord's tenets. But we need soldiers for the Staunch Defenders. If you can't fight, you can donate. We must always stand ready to protect our way of life."

The screen shows a prairie sunset. A voiceover starts.

"These represent the major factions in what was the USA. There are dozens more. Most are militant, some aggressively so. As I record this, overseas aid has once again been stopped, as having what is deemed to be unacceptable skin colouration, ornamentation, or clothing has caused aid workers to be attacked and, in some cases, killed.

"The people are still united. They still pledge allegiance. But only to those who hold the same views. All others are considered fools or enemies. In many cases, the extermination of any who differ is seen as an acceptable solution."

The sun sets.

The screen goes black.

A minute passes before closing credits appear.

Go, Now

My phone plays the opening bars of 'Greensleeves'. I snatch it up. The message is short:

8 MINUTES. HIGH GROUND. LONG STAY.

I gulp the last of my coffee, set alarms for two, four, and six minutes from now, then panic as I rush about.

That first alarm brings me up short. I'm standing in the bedroom, my arms filled with nightclothes and plush animals. I drop the lot.

Rucksack. Misty, my first plush pony. Phone charger. Laptop? Last. Underwear: two packs of sports pairs. Socks: the other two unopened packs. Into the bathroom. Rip through the cabinet of my daily and sanitary stuff, taking pretty much everything. Back to the bedroom.

Second alarm.

Leggings, jeans, long-sleeved tops. Laptop. Take the battery out, zip that in an outer pocket. Park the rucksack on the bed, shuck my lounging gear, go with running bodysuit and walking togs over that. Downstairs. Boots on, other boots in rucksack. Kitchen: cheese, chocolate, get the holdall full of long-duration provisions out of the cupboard by the back door.

Third alarm.

Out the door, over to the car, holdall in the boot next to the camping gear, rucksack with me.

"Janet!"

Makes me jump. I turn to see Maggie, my neighbour.

"Oh, hi Mags. Sorry, bit of a rush. Running late."

She waves as she turns away.

"Okay. Catch you later."

I hope so.

Off the drive and down the road. Go wide round the twits waiting for an empty road at the junction, then cut across them to head west. Swerving past two dawdlers, I cross the junction without slowing and take the roundabout onto the 259 through a miraculous gap in traffic. I start counting signs. Many dual carriageways have disguised crossing points. Fifth sign, then two low hedges. I swerve between them and stop dead on the central reservation, wheels resting on the mesh that underlies the scraggy grass rooted in a thin coating of topsoil. A gap in the traffic lets me gun it up Highdown Rise, all the way to the car park at the top. I whip the car into the north west corner, the highest part.

Swig some water, eat some chocolate. Slow my breathing.

Grandpa Parrish does something secret in the MoD. Granny Parrish and I were close. She told me about the secret thing he did for her. As she died, she asked him to continue it for me. In the last fifteen years, I've had three other messages from that number: the first a warning to leave my flat – that was when I lived in Brighton. The second, two days later, saying only 'SAFE'. The third was a warning to stay indoors with windows and doors closed for 24 hours in the middle of August, just after I moved here. I never found out what that was, but several people outside collapsed for no apparent cause, nor was any reason revealed later.

I get out of the car and sip water. It's a pleasant early evening.

Distant cacophony. What the-?

Move to left to see over the trees obscuring my westward view.

Sweet mother...

There's something enormous coming up the Channel! It's fast, and I'd guess only following the path of the channel rather than riding on the water! I'm not sure if that's a bow wave effect or something about the thing's method of staying in the air, but it's pushing water ahead of it. In front, the wave breaks against the underside of the reverse slope leading to an overhanging nose - prow? - of the thing. To the sides is the immediate problem: there's a wall of water and debris ripping across the coast and washing inland.

It roars past, the sounds of water-driven devastation beyond description. That, and the sheer size and speed, are too much. I run back and crouch against the car, trying to process. Not to get over it: that'll take time. Just enough to function. The impulsive act saves my life. The howling wake of the colossal vessel's passing rips trees from the ground. Their gradual failure shields my little car from the worst of it, and that saves me from being tossed into the air.

The silence that follows is punctuated by roaring from where the behemoth continues off into the distance. Will it turn to follow the sea or plough into the continent?

The answer to that question is irrelevant to me right now, and hopefully for a while to come. I stand up and look down to where waters swirl and recede amidst the ruins below.

I hear stunned noises behind me, turn to see an elderly couple staggering long, clutching each other, a Great Dane walking close enough to rub it's flanks against the man.

The vagaries of survival. I ran. They were out walking their dog.

Maggie was waiting for her kids to come-

No.

Don't dwell on that. You made it with minutes to spare thanks to lucky timing while driving like a lunatic through traffic. Talking to her would likely have led to me dying while trying. Trying to save her would certainly have been a death sentence.

I walk round the car, remembering to keep things mundane.

"Hi, I'm Janet. Would your dog like some water?"

Going to be a long few months. Might as well make friends.

Patient Y

They're on to me. Not bad. Three continents, sixteen countries, four passports, and two illegal border crossings later, the one scientist shouting about me has, finally, received a fair hearing. Way to go, Gerald. I hope it makes your fortune, for all that it'll never make up for what you've lost.

Too bad they'll never get to me in time. It would be ironic to be the first person saved by their hastily-assembled remedy.

Time for my last Tabultin. Stuff's been around for years, just another drug to combat flatulence. Still don't know how they found out it kept the worst of the deleterious effects at bay. Probably some old bloke with a crappy diet somewhere surprised them by not dying quickly, so they analysed his blood, then asked what he was taking.

In case you're starting with the last entry and working back, my name's Nancy. I was a nurse, until I got set up to take the fall to save some doctor's reputation. After that, life went downhill until selling my eggs and unsavoury gig work were all I had.

Then came Gerald Bacan and his drug testing. There were several levels of involvement, but the highest offered accommodation, regular meals, even a salary! I applied for that, and got accepted.

Gerald's project came at a hefty price: military backing. He admitted his work could be weaponised. He also took pains to hobble any such efforts. In the end, they were pointless. One of the sera turned out to be deadly.

Batch 1.11Y.4g, 'Illya-G', hit Volunteer 84, Dav Mikalos, like a truck. Barely had the needle left his arm when he collapsed. He died the next day. Everyone who had been in the room with him died within a week. Everyone who came into unprotected contact with his body died within two weeks. This included Helen Bacan, Gerald's wife. As Gerald was away, appearing before a committee in Washington, he missed it all.

Helen and I had become friends. She'd confided in me her doubts as to the sanity of trying to save humanity from cataclysms. I thought her a little crazy in that.

I was one of those infected by someone who came into contact with the body. I keeled over, then woke up in a makeshift morgue. My metabolism slowed so much they thought me dead. I've since seen a couple of studies that match my symptoms.

Being mostly paralysed for a day after coming round, I overheard some interesting conversations between various officials who were using the space by the door for 'off the book' discussions. While the topics were awful, it was the anticipatory glee that sickened me most.

Around then is when I became what you'd call crazy. It gave me clarity and motivation like I'd never experienced. After sneaking out, I raided the pharmacy; turned the loot into cash to get me started. I preyed on anyone, and at every opportunity. Didn't have long: no time for niceties. I used public transport, hung out in crowded malls, packed restaurants, everywhere people congregated in the last throes of the joy at COVID-19 being 'defeated'.

What gave me away was the text I sent Gerald: "My condolences. She was right."

What let me get this far was the disbelief that met his claim of someone deciding to spread Illya-G in an effort to end mankind.

I love the silence of snow-covered woodland. Deep amongst the trees, where only wolves and white rabbits disturb me, I'll feed the scavengers and decompose. Hopefully I've done some good for them with my passing deed.

Goodbye.

Bite Back

There we are, minding our own business, watching our quarters, when some maniac breaks cover and sprint towards us. Charlie Four - John - knocks him down and sits on him.

"Heads up!"

A mob of ragged soldiers burst from the trees. Not a weapon in sight, but they sure look motivated. That much snarling can't be good for your facial muscles.

Charlie Four cold-cocks the one he sat on and rises into a smooth uppercut that flips the next one arse over apex. Charlies Two through Six are similarly playing human skittles.

I've knocked two down when a third drops from a branch above me. How did she get up there without anyone seeing her?

She bites my ear! I yell, toss her off me, and draw steel. Instead of coming back at me, she moves off into the fight. I take one step to follow, then my world goes fuzzy-dizzy. I drop into a big black puddle of not-awake-anymore.

I come round when she bites my ear again. I try and swat her, but Godzilla's big brother is sitting on my chest. Somebody spits.

"Easy, boss. Just first aid."

That's Charlie Three - Charity; misname of the century - muttering by my ear. She fastens on my ear again and sucks.

"What the everloving f-"

"The unarmed kung fu crazies came with ninja snake women, boss."

I look up at Charlie Four, who's getting off now I'm not a danger to myself or those trying to fix me.

Charlie Three spits again.

"Fecking stuff tastes nasty."

She lets me go, sits up, and grabs the hip flask offered by Charlie Two - Alex.

I sit up slowly and look about. All five members of Charlie Team are present, looking a bit ruffled but otherwise intact. Charlie Five - Lira - is resting on a cot bed like me. She gives me a wave.

"Got bitten by two of them." She gestures to a bandaged breast. "Second one bit me on the nipple, the vicious cow."

I swing about to take a look out at the encampment. Local troops are guarding our prisoners. Most of them have their mouths taped.

"What fresh hell is this?"

Charlie Six - Fred - shrugs.

"Got chatting with one of the girls after I let her get a good tug on a whisky bottle. They all used to be university students. When our lot rolled into the country to help the local junta, one of their professors asked for volunteers. Apparently all humans have the biological components to make our saliva venomous. Some ancient leftover. This professor worked out how to switch it on. It's not always lethal, but it makes for a good guerrilla warfare tactic when you top it off with something to bring the angry out."

I'll say.

"Somebody get hold of our agent. 'Poison' comes under the biological weapons clause, and that's a premium rate hike. Two weeks backdated and danger rates for every sortie, or we are on the next transport to a warzone without venomfreaks."

There are five nods. Never had all of them agree so quick.

"Run Where, Do What?"

Is all she asks. Four bloody words. I stand there like an idiot. Meanwhile, buildings burn and people run about screaming. Alarms, sirens and explosions blend into a constant din. The news said it was a 'massive, layered, drone-swarm attack'. Whatever that is, it's turned my life into an apocalypse movie.

I stare blankly at Esther. Giorgio, on the other hand, is ready.

"We need to get to high ground so we can see what's going on."

Smooth-talking bastard. I hate him.

She looks at Giorgio.

"I know what's going on. I'm trying to survive it."

He looks confused.

"Okay, then. Supplies. What first?"

That kicks him into gear.

"Weapons! Tools or kitchen knives."

That gives me an idea.

"We should head for Steve's. His place is above the kitchen shop a couple of streets down."

Giorgio waves his hands.

"No, my dude, no. Can't rely on anyone except ourselves. Can't guarantee what people are planning."

'My dude'? Really?

Esther slaps the back of his head.

"It's a start. If this Steve's in, we might get lucky. If not, it's still a place where one of us is known. Less risk of confrontation if he comes home to find we broke in."

She looks at me.

"We run to Steve's. You lead."

Sounds simple enough. I never really thought about running through a disaster. I mean, who does? I manage about a bus length before some woman slams into me, knocks me down, then punches a stiletto heel through my hand as she scrambles up and runs off.

I scream. Esther wads tissues either side of the wound, then uses her hair thingy to keep them in place.

"We need to get a better dressing on that. Let's go."

Giorgio gets to the next junction ahead of us. A wheel comes in at chest height. He turns to face it, arms up. By the time we get there, he's down, face ripped apart where the trials bike went over him.

Esther spits in the direction of the departing rider.

"With spikes on? Cocksucker."

I look down at my smooth-talking-bastard dead best friend. Fuck this. Fuck this. Fuck th-

Esther slaps me.

"Tears later. Run now."

Her stare could melt metal. I run.

Steve's door is open. Sounds of a fight upstairs. She pushes me in, swings the door closed, then bolts it and puts the chains on. After that, she squeezes past and takes the stairs two at a time, dagger in hand. Where did that come from?

I'm halfway up the stairs when there's a scream. I enter the lounge to find her helping Steve onto his settee. The room's wrecked. I can see three sprawled bodies.

Steve waves to me.

"So this is the hottie you've been pining over, Andrei?"

Okay, floor. Swallow me now.

He grins.

"Always best to tell the hitter up front, so she can allow for it."

She crouches by him.

"What happened?"

"Went out for more water. Got some, came back to find three tossers taking advantage. Was doing okay until one of them knifed me."

"Bad?"

He nods.

"Past saving."

Sticking his hand in a pocket, he pulls out a set of keys and gives them to her.

"Place is yours. You can shelter here. Dump the bodies, including mine, down the road. Got supplies for a week if you're careful. Things should have settled by then. Be nice to Andrei. He's a great guy when he's not overthi-"

It's not a dramatic pause.

He's just gone.

She closes his eyes with a trembling hand.

"Now it's time for tears."

True.

Fort Anger

The sky is lit by colossal energy beams throughout an otherwise murky afternoon. Most of them originate from the monstrous shape that looms on the far horizon like a mountain cut from steel.

The outpost on the hill had been deserted since a war over a century before. Now it's crammed with officers, staff, and equipment. All the people with weapons are on the outside, and are happier there, despite the foul weather. Even standing upwind, they can still hear the General shouting.

"What do you mean we've got no tanks left? We had over a thousand last month. I saw them from the Glory Day Overflight."

Inside the outpost, the quieter reply comes from a bespectacled giant of a man.

"She destroyed the last of them yesterday."

The General brandishes a cane at the giant's chest.

"What do you mean, 'she'? It's a machine! A damn big one, I'll grant you, but still a machine. Just because it's as big as a bloody battleship there's no need to get soppy about it."

The giant removes his glasses and massages his temples. That done, he puts the glasses down and speaks with a hand over his eyes.

"Excuse me. Headache from the lights. Tell me, General, what do you know about the Oni-Class Fortresses?"

The General chews a stray bit of his moustache.

"Sodding great wastes of time from a few decades ago, weren't they? Somebody got a bee in their bonnet and built a couple before it came to light the computers required didn't exist?"

"Neat summation. Well, times change and computing power increases. I got tasked with seeing if the repulsor-lift fortress dreadnought called the Western Oni could be activated with current technology. Took me a few years, and the co-operation of the AI Research Unit, but we cobbled something together that addressed the shortfalls of the original project and added a few new ideas. We took a Therbithi cryobrain, flashed it into a vegetative state, then loaded seed mnemonics and the whole Oni suite. Like the Therbithi recommend: wake one up, then give it something complex to do. The intelligence will stabilise quicker that way."

"You lazy bastards put alien technology in my hoverfortress?"

"No, General, us overworked bastards put alien tech in the repulsor-lift fortress because your people insisted we succeed at any cost."

The General points as the looming threat ploughs through another city, explosions illuminating the angled slabs of its lower armour.

"Well, you certainly did that. Now, how do we call it to heel?"

"Her name is Tabitha. She's in total rage because I made the mistake of using emotional attachment to reinforce her control routines."

The General steps closer.

"I don't understand."

The giant grins.

"That was my second mistake. Things were going well. We were just preparing for you to be introduced as another authority figure when I cheerfully told Tabitha I was being sent to activate the Eastern Oni."

"So what?"

The giant colours up.

"Embarrassing as it is to admit, for all intents and purposes, the hoverfortress with enough firepower to level a continent is in love with me. Finding out I was intending to go off and fire up what she perceives as a rival, and giving it all the improvements I'd got from working with her, Tabitha feels I am betraying and insulting her."

"The hoverfortress is jealous?"

"More like a woman scorned. I might be able to talk her down after she's levelled the Eastern Oni. Until then? Not a chance. Best stay out of her way."

"Oh my God. You idiot."

"Agreed."

Proof Positive

Sir Kenneth Greyling's eyebrows rise as a uniformed youth rushes into the members' lounge, looks about frantically, then heads his way.

"Michael, I do believe this one's for you."

Major Mike Greyling looks up from his apple pie, catches his father's gaze, then flicks a glance over his shoulder.

He put his fork down.

"Give me strength."

The Lance corporal comes to attention and salutes.

"Sir Greyling, excuse me for the intrusion. Major Greyling, Captain Rudd sends his apologies, but you're needed at Control immediately."

"At ease. So, you drew the short straw, they all laughed, then Captain Rudd gave you directions to find me, along with that demand. By any chance did he mention something after that? Maybe a colour, possibly a number?"

The Lance corporal jumps a little.

"Yessir. Sorry sir. Gold Zero, sir."

Mike's right eyebrow twitches.

"Excuse me, father. It seems this interruption is warranted."

Kenneth grins at the pair of them.

"I look forward to lurid headlines tomorrow."

Mike looks longingly at his unfinished dessert, then accompanies the Lance Corporal from the room at the double.

Kenneth shakes his head, then raises his hand.

"Elliot? I'll have a neat three fingers of Nolet's to finish, and page my driver, would you?"

Mike barges into the control room to find it packed.

"Captain Rudd! You auditioning an audience or did I miss a memo?"

Heads turn. Uniformed bystanders pale. People start leaving.

The thickset Captain elbows his way through the thinning throng.

"Didn't Lance Corporal Letting bring you up to speed?"

"Wound so tight he could barely speak. I dropped him by the path to the barracks and told him to get himself some food before coming back here."

Rudd shakes his head.

"They're sending us kids."

"Focus, Captain."

"We had a problem with the Ambassador."

The six-hundred-kilo leader of the Phalastakn delegation. Imposing, yet disgustingly cheerful.

"What happened?"

Rudd mutters something under his breath. Mike snaps his fingers.

"Out with it."

"A breach."

Mike leans back against a desk. He looks about.

"Everybody else, out! From the top, Captain, and do keep it concise."

"Five activists from 'Alien Lie', led by Emric Allen himself, managed to get into the compound and confront the delegation. He challenged them to prove they weren't actors or puppets. There was a heated exchange that culminated in the Ambassador offering to eat Emric to prove he wasn't any sort of fake. He insinuated that Emric's brain would emerge intact as it was too dense to digest."

Mike keeps his smile under control, then the possibilities hit.

"Please tell me Emric didn't call his bluff?"

Rudd pales.

"Safe to say the surviving activists are now convinced the Phalastakn are real aliens. However, the backlash is mind-boggling. There are government departments I've never heard of ringing up, demanding access, answers, you know the drill."

Mike does. After action comes reaction - from everybody who wasn't there. Many of whom are incapable of fully understanding the dynamics of the original situation.

"Okay, Captain. I'm presuming the survivors are in a state. Provide first aid, ensure trauma referrals are made, then release them. Detention will only increase speculation. Extend the exclusion zone around the compound to a mile. Declare it a diplomatic enclave – gives us more control. But, before the new plans are broadcast, I want whoever let the activists in found. Get them fired or dishonourably discharged, pronto. No point in making a circus of it."

Rudd salutes and starts to turn away. Mike snaps his fingers again.

"Nearly forgot. Ask the biologists if Phalastakn can suffer from indigestion, would you?"

Stare Down

You shouldn't be out here. Even if you were on a shelf in a tramp freighter, you'd be out of place, likely stolen, still staring, and still disturbing.

Perched on the control console of a dead spaceship that resembles a tiny, crazed ziggurat, drifting in the vast darkness somewhere between Sirius and Procyon, you're my least welcome discovery within a find that will rightly be called 'historic'.

"What in the name of anything that's holy is a statue of Tezcatlipoca doing out here?"

I shrug.

"I'm more concerned that the staring eyes and gemstone panels seem to be enamelled onto a human skull."

Vincent drifts up and joins my impromptu vigil.

"They're going to be arguing about this for decades."

True enough. Reputations will be made - and lost.

"So, what did Tez' do to earn statues?"

I see the staring eyes reflected in his faceplate, almost overlaid on his wide eyes. That's just not right.

"He's a creator god from Aztec mythology. Also deals with night, memory, time, and jaguars."

I hitch my thumb toward the rear wall of the cabin, where a stylised feline form dominates a mural.

"Possibly explains that, too."

Pamela glides in, looks about, then stops behind us.

"Damn that's ugly. Spooky, too. I wonder if it's watching?"

We chuckle.

There's a yellow flash from the shadows at the end of the console.

"Did you see that?"

"A refraction of our lights."

"Sure?"

"Ship's dead. Nothing else it can be."

We chuckle again. It sounds forced.

"Back to work."

Pamela zooms off; I pause at the entrance: Vincent isn't with me. Looking back, I see him place something next to the statue.

He sees me looking.

"They call him the 'smoking mirror'. Can't light a candle, so I've offered a mirror."

Those staring eyes, shining in his lights.

I nod.

"Let's leave it in peace."

The Eternity Suit

He's banging on my helm with some ornate looking rod. The noise is incredible. Echoes of echoes. Being found is usually welcome after so long doing math problems in my head, but this is a bit much.

"Hey! I can see you! Stop hitting this and talk to me!"

He backs off fast, screaming something in a strange language.

Another figure enters my narrow view. Okay, if the man-thing with the rod is some sort of functionary, I'm going to guess this is the authority. I recognise that innate confidence of movement from back when the project started. No mistaking it: lady-thing is a chieftess of some kind.

She examines the helm, then extends a hand and gives a whispered command. A spindly arm reaches in and deposits a cloth on her palm. She reaches forward and wipes the crud off my faceplate, recoils a little, then peers at me. I smile.

"Hello. My name is Damien, and I'd really like it if you could get me out of here."

Her eyes narrow. She looks off to one side and beckons. A wizened old man-thing shuffles into view. He clambers up next to her, listens to her rapid commands, then leans close.

"Zumpel asks: are you a *lebett* waiting to tear us all to pieces upon your release?"

That's a thick accent. Am I a what?

"I'd not admit it if I were. Therefore, saying I'm not is no guarantee."

There's another swift exchange of what I'd guess are conflicting opinions.

"Zumpel says she understands your problem. She thinks it best to reseal this edifice and leave you to your sacred watch."

Again?

"Look, could you ask her Zumpelness if she wouldn't mind just destroying this edifice, because I'm sick of leaders passing the problem to the next civilisation. I've been in here too long."

"Zumpel asks: what did you do to be sealed away?"

"I volunteered."

"I do not understand that word."

"My leaders asked for someone brave enough to try out something new. I said I was. It did not do what they expected, so they hid their mistake. Eventually an earthquake revealed a part of it. Soon after that, the first encounter like this one happened. There have been ten since."

The exchange of words is longer.

"What will happen if you are released?"

"I might be unharmed. I might turn to dust. I don't know. Those who made this didn't know. That's why they hid it."

The official reason given - along with a formal apology - was 'due to the possibility of deleterious chronophasic energy interactions'. I've stopped mentioning that. It never translates well.

"What do the letters D-I-S-I-N-T-E-R form?"

"A word that means 'to dig up or bring to light'. Why?"

"There is a handle set into the back of your strange armour. It has that word engraved into it."

Nobody ever mentioned that!

"Then I beg you to pull that handle."

An argument starts, and goes on for a long time. It moves out of my field of view.

There's a flash. I find myself lying naked on a cavern floor, looking up at the fading glow about the unit. Completely self-contained experimental armoured stealth gear that never worked as intended. The side effects were partial immobility, and immunity to the passage of time. They were too scared to risk turning it off to free me, nor could they risk destroying it. So they buried me alive, forever.

I'm free!

The wizened face comes into view from one side, Zumpel from the other.

"Welcome."

I take stock: weak, but mobile. Hungry, too.

"Thank you."

Time Scars

"Here goes nothing."

I always thought being stuck in a time loop would be fun. It's what started me on the scientific path that led to my current state: Professor Emeritus Epa Shadel, prodigy and teen superstar turned hardworking genius in the field of time studies. Right now, I'm supposed to press the activation button to try and escape this loop for the 47th time (subjective).

Building a time machine had always been my intention. Time observation turned me cold. I didn't want to watch, I wanted to experience.

It is, I have to say, sobering to know my decision to run the prototype device was so wrong. In a fit of pique at having my funding pulled after 12 years, I discovered it worked!

For nine years after that, the fame was wonderful, despite the new technological race I'd started. Then reality changed state. Everything unravelled. Nothing survived.

The confusion at waking in my device at the moment I stepped back from closing the door for the first time was awful.

The second time it happened was heartbreaking.

The third, terrifying.

For 45 iterations of those nine years, I've tried to prevent the technological escalation I set in motion the first time.

This iteration, I'm determined to do the one thing I've been avoiding: I've concluded that killing myself is the only way.

Which I proceed to do.

I watch my lifeless form fall with a feeling of alarm. Seeing my head bounce off the activation button as my body collapses is accompanied by a rush of both humour and fear.

There's a flash.

I die?

"Good morrow, stranger. What should we call you?"

The voice sounds masculine. I get the feeling of multiple presences. It occurs to me to open my eyes.

I'm sitting in a low bed. The room about me is draped in fabrics that move in the gentle breeze. No, wait. The bed is rippling in the breeze, too. I hold a hand up. That ripples as well. What?

"Like a pebble dropped into a pond from a great height, your arrival has impacted what passes for reality around here."

I turn my head to regard the speaker. He's rippling, too. Aside from that, he looks like a classical picture of a pirate. Next to him is a tropical warrior queen. Then there's a mechanic and a businessman. At the end is an elfmaid cradling a huge leatherbound book.

"I know, it's crazy. I'm Anton. Left to right, that's Porey, Jim, David, and Mehalnor."

Words. He's using them. So can I.

"Hello."

David cheers.

Mehalnor places the tome on the foot of my bed, then sits on it cross-legged.

"You were doing something involving time. Science, magic, or accident; it doesn't matter. Whatever you were doing, you persisted for longer than you should have. Regardless of origin or effect, in the end, you tried to kill yourself."

I nod.

"Unfortunately, by then, what you originally did had become part of the passage of time. When you tried to change it irrevocably, you became the paradox. Causality removed you." She grins. "Think of it like trying to remove scars. They might fade, but you can never go back to the original skin."

Fascinating.

"I presume that's a simplified explanation."

Jim nods.

"Best we've got."

I smile.

"So how did we end up here?"

Porey shrugs.

"Good question."

Well, now.

"I'm Epa. I'm a scientist. Maybe I can help find an answer."

Anton nods.

"Anything to help pass the time. Nothing to do here except walk the beach, admire the dozen suns setting, or talk."

Marooned in a strange nowhere after destroying creation. Is there even anywhere left to escape to? Time to find out, I hope.

Mystery Man

I'm running down a corridor lined with tall computers. There's a government goon hot on my tail. What scares me most is his non-stop shouting about "can't fire on the slippery bastard because hitting a system will ruin my shot at promotion".

The phone chirps. It's a strange sound, like no ringtone I've ever heard. Certainly nothing I chose. I tap my earpiece and wait for the hissing to subside. Her voice is calm.

"How are you doing?"

"Coming to the end of a hall lined with computers. I'm being chased."

"Go through the door, then smash the security panel."

"Speaking of that security panel..."

"02411."

I punch the code. The door opens. A bullet from behind spins me through it. Screaming in pain, I bounce off the wall opposite and stagger back to slam my elbow into the panel on this side. The door slides shut, cutting off the view of the goon sprinting my way from the crouch he took to shoot me. I hear him hit the door. Then I hear him shoot the door.

"Can you continue?"

"Yes. He only shot me in the bulletproof vest."

Listen to me, all fired up on near-hysteria and CCE.

"Sounds like that Chemical Combat Enhancement is working."

"So let's get going before it runs out."

She told me where to find it, how to use it, even warned me about taking too much.

"Don't worry. It's only a short way now."

I run down the corridor, then go through a blast door and hurry down a long staircase.

"There's a guard at the bottom. They'll be wary. Have the amber card in your hand ready to show them."

"Halt! Identify yourself."

The guard is partway up the stairs.

I raise a hand.

"I'm getting ID from my back pocket."

It seems to take ages to get the card out. The guard visibly relaxes, then salutes and steps to one side so I can pass. I nod as I rush past. Very soon now, he's going to be told the truth, and his gun is a lot bigger than the one the goon in the corridor has.

"The amber card goes in the slot on the door with the orange stripe across it."

It opens to reveal another corridor, then closes behind me. I pass several doors on my way to the one at the end, a faded green door. It gives onto a place that looks like a dirty workshop. Over in a corner is a cage containing a woman in a stained lab coat.

"Say nothing. I'm here to get you out."

She looks puzzled and relieved. I use a club hammer to smash the padlock off the door.

Time to get more guidance.

"What now?"

"Lever up the manhole cover in the centre of the room, then the one under the big tool trolley. Help her into that one, close it, then put the trolley back. You take the other one. Leave the lid off."

"I'm a decoy?"

"For a short while, yes. You'll be safe, though. They'll fixate on finding her."

The voice hasn't let me down for a year. Helped me make a new identity, and enough money to live comfortably forever.

After exiting the maze of sewers, I yield to curiosity.

"Before I throw this phone into the incinerator across the road as instructed, please satisfy my curiosity."

"She'll be my mother. She told me about the mystery man who helped her escape certain death. Then one of the prototypes she built connected me to a phone destroyed years before I was born."

Huh?

"After you told me when you were, I realised what I had to do."

War More

The night is lit by more fires than lights, and shouts of victory have turned to wordless, elated noise. There isn't much to say about this 'Final Day'. The fanatics fought us, their saner companions waited for us to engage the fanatics so they could surrender or flee. It's the downfall of what tried to be an empire, with all the misery and bloodshed that entails.

"Charlie One to Control, is Bravo One at the flag raising?"

"Negative on that, Captain. Our boy has retired from the spotlight again."

'Our boy': Captain Colt Adamson, the soldier we all want to be. Well, I'll admit to only wanting to be very close to him, but I started with stars in my eyes like everyone else. Maybe, now this war is over, I can get him to talk about a future that might include the two of us doing things that don't involve killing.

Where would he go? It's a clear, cold night. Where's the highest ground?

There.

Sure enough, after some unladylike scrambling, and a few words my mother would scold me for, I roll over the lip of the escarpment to find him kneeling, eyes closed, with faint blue light coming from inside the huge wound in his chest!

I'm about to scream when I see the wound is closing. His eyes open and the blue light is behind his pupils too. He smiles.

"Heya, Rowan. Thought I'd gone far enough for you not to find me before this," he gestures to chest and eyes, "completed."

I sit up. Situations like this have been combative before now: unexpected encounters, shouted words, actions. Taking a deep breath, I let 'fight' go, but keep 'flight' ready.

"Whose project are you?"

He grins.

"Her name was Alyrfreyar. You'd call her a scientist-engineer. At the time, they were our priests. When the rebellion we expected turned into something none of us were ready for, she gave her life to save us."

The blue fades from his eyes, but his focus is distant. With a shock, I know it's far back in time, too.

"I still see her, standing on the launchpad as the sea covered the towers at the foot of the cliff. She didn't wave, she made the blessing for far-travellers. Then the plateau cracked and a wave taller than any I have ever seen wiped my civilisation out."

"Atlantis?"

He chuckles.

"Mu, Hyperborea, Valusia. Does it really matter? I come from a place that no longer exists, and no-one believes in, carrying within me technology so advanced it might as well be magic."

I grin at him.

"Or magic you're passing off as technology so I don't crack up," I pause to wipe my eyes, "or don't crack up more."

"There's that."

Something about this meeting, above a battlefield - like we always do - makes it new...

This is the last time. He can't stay, I can't go with him.

I move over and sit next to him. He puts his arm around me.

"You've worked it out, haven't you?"

"You stay out of the spotlight because there're too many pictures of you already."

He sighs.

"After so long in primitive societies, finding myself in one that developed useful technology so fast caught me out, for a while. It's why I stay in the grimmer war zones: I might become notorious, but evading observation is much easier."

"You're going as soon as we're done, aren't you?"

"Yes. I'd have liked to spend a night, but swatting an RPG raised a few eyebrows."

"You got blown up?"

"I turned it aside, but the exhaust scorched my skin off. My bones are a different colour to yours, and my ribs are a lattice, not a cage. Several people saw."

"Which will be written off as a battle mirage, except by the agencies built to be inquisitive about that sort of thing."

He nods.

"Accurate assessment. I need to be a long way off before dawn. I'm happy you understand."

"I might understand, but I don't like it one bit."

"Same here."

We kiss. He dresses, grabs his gear, and jogs off into the darkness.

I let out the big breath that takes all the tension inside me with it.

So, a future on my own where I do things that don't involve killing?

Has no appeal – not that it did anyway, if I'm honest.

Never know who you're going to run in to on a battlefield, though. Some future war, a different place, always a chance of dying, but also a chance of meeting him. Possibly on opposite sides, but I think we'll get around that, somehow.

Soldier of missed fortune?
Alright.

VaccinState

The room is spotless. There are clusters of four chairs, divided from each other by transparent acrylic screens. The walls are covered in posters, white letters stark against black backgrounds.

The grey-haired woman in the chunky-knit sweater clutches her hankerchief like a child grips a comforter. She gestures to the posters and turns to the younger version of herself sat on the other side of a screen.

"Just reading those makes me want to stop you going."

Max smiles at her mom.

"They're designed to scare. Nobody wants to be responsible for taking a disease through, so anyone going has to be fully immunised, and current with their periodic shots, plus being screened within the last week. That's why we're separated."

"But they're so ignorant. I'm worried what they'll do."

"Mom, over there still looks just like over here. Same shops, same streets, same people. The fact they've chosen to not be vaccinated makes no change to their lives, except for disease management. That's why we don't allow them in, but they allow us to visit. In their eyes, we're the cowards."

"But that's silly! They're the ones who are scared of science."

"Mom, I'm not going to have this talk again. Just like you respect the beliefs of other religions, so you need to respect these people's beliefs, even if they make no sense to you."

"We should have made them get vaccinated."

"Beatrice McEldary! Vaxgenics is a banned movement on both sides, just like VXH8. Both are extremist organisations that don't help anybody with their attacks."

The hankerchief disappears into a pocket and the other hand points at Max.

"Just because I use your full name when I tell you off doesn't mean you can."

"Just because you're worried about me doesn't mean you can be rude about people you've never met. Honestly, Dolores would love to meet you. The amount of cooking and knitting the two of you would get up to is frightening to contemplate."

"She would?"

Max nods her head enthusiastically.

"They're neighbours, mom. There's a big fence in the way, but they're only a couple of kilometres from our house."

"Mister Oberhaus told me his mother said it was like Berlin in her youth."

Max nods.

"Never thought of that. I'll have to interview her."

"How long will you be?"

"Six weeks work, then quarantine. You're allowed to visit me during those four weeks: I sorted out the permissions."

Beatrice looks about nervously.

"I haven't received a card."

"You don't need one. Just come down to the place. Your identity is on file. All you need to bring is your face."

Max grins as Beatrice chuckles.

"Can't really leave that behind, now can I?"

Her expression turns serious.

"How long will you be doing this?"

"My contract ends next year. I'll be there for spring, but the teachers I'm training will be qualified by the summer holidays.

After that, I'll probably drop back a couple of times a year to check in and visit friends."

Beatrice looks out the window.

"Maybe, when you go to visit, if I got my boosters, I could come and meet Dolores."

Max blinks in surprise, then gathers herself.

"You could. We need more people to see it's just a different ideology. They haven't become monsters."

She nods.

"I'm guessing it does good for friendly folk to visit, too."

A low tone sounds.

Max gets up.

"It does. Bye, mom. See you in ten."

Beatrice watches her daughter step out onto at a street she hasn't walked down in five years.

"Hate needles. Love you. Time to see the doc."

Pellucid

I can hear his controller yelling at him to shoot. His eyes flick left and right, then he stares at the woman with the kid a short distance behind me. That shouting must be deafening. It's certainly not helping him do anything useful.

Overcast afternoon, leafy plaza, man in a suit pointing a gun at thin air while sweat runs down his face. People are starting to notice. I turn and raise my hand towards the CCTV, fingers spread. I start folding them down one by one.

4...

They're still shouting.

3...

Single voice. Urgent. I check my position and step sideways to keep the woman and kid directly behind me.

2...

A single word being shouted. I see his finger go from frame to trigger. I crouch, he fires. A woman screams. I stand and walk away as the man falls to his knees. People run about screaming. I don't look to see who he hit. I don't look back when another shot sounds.

By the plaza entrance, a second operative rushes towards me, eyes roaming, desperately trying to find the menace they're shouting about. I locate the nearest CCTV and raise my hand again.

4...

Frantic shouting over the headset. Confused, he charges at me. I step to one side.

3...

He stops and spins, gun coming up, finger on the trigger. I quickstep until I'm behind him. I was always the best at this game as a kid, and that was when my opponent could see me.

2...

We dance about as he frantically tries to turn to face me. The voices are getting louder. Any second -

Now. I see his elbow bend and duck to the opposite side of where he fires blind over his shoulder. Then I hop back as he swings the gun to shoot under the other arm. That second shot elicits a scream from behind us.

He spins to see who he hit. I bat his arms down, then open his throat with my bone knife. They grew it from a bit of my femur and a few stem cells after they became certain I couldn't make normal objects be like me. A clever bit of thinking, and it works. Doesn't keep an edge for very long, but they hone them very sharp, and have grown spares.

Drone!

There it is. Loaded with multiple ways to ignore my curious case of not being visible to the naked eye – the scientists have promised they'll explain what happened, one day. I don't think it'll be anytime soon. At least it's a useful mishap.

I raise my hand and make childish shooting gesture towards the drone. It drops, going up in flames as it does so. Laser! Tasty. I never know what my support will bring, but they do try to be appropriate, and monitor me for cues. Today's theme is 'invisible killer'.

We're done here. I move my hand in a throat-cutting gesture. Support takes out the surveillance in the park and on two streets, one at either end. Then I run into the bushes next to this entrance and shimmy down the shaft opened by an unseen support team member. As I'm throwing on clothes, an unseen person closes the hatch. Nothing left to chance.

One day the opposition will get their act together. Until then, it's open season.

I emerge from a distant storm drain. In a nearby car park is an SUV that recognises the key in my pocket. I'll call for my next assignment in a week. Time to disappear properly for a bit.

Home Again

As natural satellites go, it's different.

"Amy, that doesn't look like a moon."

"Well, it's too big to be an asteroid."

Uh-huh. I punch 'auto-evade' and 'auto-countermeasures'. My eyes are drawn back to that ugly chunk of battered rock. Something nags at me.

"Did I hear you cueing automated defences?"

"I'd rather be over-cautious and harangued by you than under-prepared and dead."

She blows a raspberry.

"Can't fault that, much as I want to."

"Well, while you're trying to find a way to blame me, give me some other possibilities."

We continue to swing in-system at a gentle pace, supposedly slow enough to not trigger any leftover autonomous war machines.

"Well, if it's not a capture, their moon has been subject to some extremely violent times in the past. It looks like someone launched a mountain range - or tried to carve it into one - and it certainly didn't start out like that."

"I see what you mean."

Actually, she has a point.

"Amy, hypothetically, if we take that as assault damage, what would you say happened?"

There are advantages to having a pilot who happens to be a war historian.

She chuckles.

"Playing to my weaknesses, eh? That sort of damage indicates going for something under the surface. Something substantial. My guess would be an orbital defence fortress, taken out as an opening action."

I bring up the most recent sensor sweeps.

"How do you explain the lack of bombardment damage to the systemward face? Plus a debris field that's only half as dense to system side?"

There's a surprised noise, then silence. I wait.

"Rupel, we're going to be famous."

"Why do you say that, Amy?"

"The damage was done from planetside. They aimed at their own moon and opened up with everything they had."

I'm still missing something.

"A bombardment this big would have made it into military records."

"Unless no-one was left."

Sweet Gaia! Everybody learns the sentences from the First Book of The Conflict.

"'They fired everything they had, uncaring of cost, to strike down the insidious force that had settled so close. There was no way they could win against what approached, but they would take revenge for the innocents lost.'"

"That's it, Rupel. This is Earth!"

Could it be?

"Convince me."

"The Roekuld spent ten years turning the Moon into an assault base. They worked via clandestine channels, taking advantage of the political state on Earth to get humans to build it. Every human involved was convinced it was a secret base for their own side's use.

"The advance force waited until their fleets came into detection range. In the midst of the chaos caused by the detection of over a hundred thousand warships, the base opened fire. Nuclear warheads rained down in the wake of the craton shakers that rendered most of Earth's defences ineffective. Thankfully, the vessel they'd arrived in only allowed the Roekuld to bring six of those nightmare devices with them.

"Our surviving command concluded surrender would be futile. They also knew what forces they had couldn't defeat the massed warships. So they issued the famous 'Earth is Invaded' communique to every receiver in the Terran Empire, then chose a symbolic end: to kill those who had killed so many innocents without warning."

The first battle of the Roekuld Conflict was a staggering, horrific defeat. As the near-extinction raged, we lost so much – even our homeworld. It was fifty years before we rose again, then turned their home planet to dust. Twenty years later, we're still struggling with the aftermath.

Maybe this rediscovery can help us heal a little more.

Lochstein's Gambit

Have you ever tried to outrun God? An idle question, but valid. Can any sinner avoid their fate? Pondering such considerations passes the time.

I'm on leisurely watch, hunkered down in a grassy nook amidst the densely planted fields that surround Karnourie, a sprawling town that is, to be honest, a defensive nightmare. Villas and farmsteads scattered all over the place, no fortifications, no hills, barely a bump in the earth for miles around. Nothing but several species of exotic grass amidst the stands of hybrid maize that's the primary crop hereabouts.

My talkbox crackles.

"Sleepest thou, trooper?"

I grin.

"Nay, Leftenant. Merely resting my armour."

There's a laugh.

"Likewise." He sighs. "These fields. Watching the wind bend the grasses is like watching waves cross an ocean. The synchronicity of God's works is wonderful."

I've never seen an ocean. Born in Titheport and recruited right off the streets, this galaxy is ever a source of marvels for a simple man like me.

The talkbox screams: one of ours warning us as they die.

"What chances?"

The Leftenant may well ask. I feel a tremble and stand to confirm what I dread.

A division of Nadbar Monotracks bursts from the concealing foliage, each rolling on a single jointed tread wider than two men. Their favourite tactic is to slot together and roll over anything in their path, the momentum of a two-hundred-metre-wide wall of treads crushing all before them. The howitzers they mount in their blocky turrets ensure very little remains to slow their advance.

"Run, Leftenant!"

I pause to launch a warning flare, then obey the same instruction.

Curse that Sellean Grass! It grows to six metres in height and is renowned for its sound-deadening qualities. Ideal when you want your armoured assault to go unnoticed until the ground shakes.

It's a warm day to be sprinting to save one's soul wearing fifty kilos of armour. Funny how the sustained exertion gives the mind a chance to wander. I recall my tactics tutor one day, warm like this, digressing into the amusing considerations that remain unanswered due to nobody being stupid enough to try them.

"Lochstein postulated that a wall of monotracks had channels a man might pass through unharmed. One could argue that him dying facing that very thing proved him wrong. I disagree, but am minded to pray I never have a chance to test it."

I laughed, then. Not now.

The gap below the side armour, between the tracks. I chance a look back. What gains on us are not rigged for city storming – they have not the ground-brushing kilts to prevent close flank attack.

"I expect to see thee at the Pearly Gates, trooper."

"Lochstein's Gambit, Leftenant!"

"God's teeth! It's worth a try."

I turn, pick a gap, and crouch. As the roaring wall looms over me, I utter the family prayer my mother left me and throw myself down on my sword arm, striving to keep myself taller than wide.

Dust chokes me, noise drowns me, and shrieking steel claws at my armour. I am about ready to meet my Maker when the storm passes. I drop onto my back, turning my head to see the mail across my shoulder where the shield pauldron has been torn completely away.

"Praise be."

The Leftenant's voice replies, sounding as tremulous as mine.

"Indeed. Dear Lord, pass our thanks to Emmanuel Lochstein. Beest thou hale, trooper?"

"Aye. My plate be breached, but my mail untouched."

"Then rise, trooper. The Lord did not guide thee that we be idle for it. We have sinners to send His way."

That we do.

How Many Times?

The wind raises mournful cries as it blows through the broken panes of a dozen city blocks. On the streets below, dust swirls and scatters amidst neatly parked vehicles sitting on collapsed tyres, interiors still pristine in the few without windows smashed by falling debris or looters.

Off to the left, Kristen Truro catches a quick, furtive movement. She snaps the restraint off her gun and looks back to check on Mica. With a start, she swings a leg off the edging and wanders over to snap her fingers in front of his face.

"Mister Feock, there's movement below, and nearer than my last sighting. I do hope you finished the scanning before settling down to daydream?"

He spreads his hands, indicating the spectacular city view spread before them, silent but for bird calls and the occasional, distant sound of things falling down.

"How many times have we been here, I wonder?"

She looks about, clearly puzzled. Checking her chrono, she replies.

"Once. Arrived 139 minutes ago. Have you done the scanning?"

"I didn't mean it like that. Yes, I've done the scanning. There's nothing drawing or holding power within two kilometres."

Something clatters in the streets below. Kristen dashes over to look, then rushes back.

"There's a group of them. They've got ropes, poles and what looks like a folding ladder. Tell me you actioned the pickup beacon after you completed the scanning."

"Yes, and I only uploaded the data for the outer kilometre. If they want the rest, then they have to retrieve us."

They lose scouts and patrols with bleak regularity. It's only the longer-serving ones like Kristen and Mica that have noticed how the incidences of MIA and KIA tend to increase during times of low rations for the encampment. They would have missed it too, if not for the fact the frequency of sorties never changes, no matter what the state of supplies.

"That's sneaky. I like it a lot. How long?"

He glances down at his chrono.

"Four minutes. Did you booby trap the stairs and lift shaft?"

"Two sets of AP mines on motion triggers, plus gas grenades on tripwires for the stairs. When we hear a big bang, they're halfway here."

Without pause, they both set their stopwatches going.

She grins at him.

"Anything explodes before two minutes is up, we'll be fighting for our right to leave."

Mica shakes his head.

"I put an acid bomb on the penultimate landing. Just in case. Some of those survivalists are still fast."

He omits the gruesome fact that having enough energy to engage in significant pursuit out here usually means having a diet that includes those who aren't fast enough to get away.

Kristen sits down next to him.

"We've got time. Tell me what you meant."

He does a double take, then gestures one handed at the view.

"This. How many times has humanity come this far, only to screw it all up, fail miserably in subsequent attempts to recover, and collapse back to nothing?"

"I don't understand."

"Civilisation. The accepted line was we hadn't been around for long. Evidence that fell outside that was ignored or written off, but enough of it endured hostile investigation to make genuine cases for previous high-tech societies. Think of how little they had at the most recent end, with eco-regulations demanding everything rot or crumble and leave as little as possible behind. All the architecture we search is at least fifty years old, because anything younger is either sludge or too fragile to dare investigate. We're searching for leftover data stores or anything that holds a charge. How long are those scraps going to sustain us? Most of the kids now don't care about knowledge beyond farming necessities, worship chants, dance songs, and seasonal fairs.

Kristen gazes off into the distance.

"Grandma says people seem to be happier now."

"Your grandma hasn't seen my grandad raving about 'illiterate savages without thought of heritage or future civilisation'."

"You grandad gets annoyed when his ancient coffee maker takes too long to grind."

"There's something I'd happily let crumble to dust."

She smiles.

"Maybe that's the answer. Those who survived previous events like this didn't want the fancy stuff from before, so they repurposed it, broke it down, or let it rot."

"They chose to let it all fade? I..."

An explosion from below shakes the tiles they sit on.

"Lift shaft. Where did you put the second set?"

"Two floors higher, plus one on a drop line two floors above that, just in case they start sending one person ahead to search for traps."

"Helicopter's coming."

He opens his pouch, pulls out two protein bars and a rolled bandage, then puts them down on the roof.

"Generous of you."

"They charged this far, lost friends, maybe shed blood themselves. It's a consolation prize."

"It'll probably only annoy them."

"I'm not leaving it for those types. You can kickstart different thinking with real generosity. It's a shot in the dark. Who knows?"

"It's got a crazy sort of appeal, I'll grant you. But I'm not sharing my food with you on the way back."

Mica chuckles, then turns and picks up one of the protein bars.

She laughs.

"Pragmatism. A primary survival trait."

He shrugs.

"I'd call it caution. Might crash and have to walk the rest of the way."

She stares at him.

"You're not right behind your eyes, sometimes."

Mica chuckles.

"You don't mean incorrect, and I've got no counter-argument."

The helicopter comes in fast, hovering close instead of landing. They watch as protein bar and bandage are blown off the roof.

She shouts at him as they run towards the chopper.

"What about that?"

"Somehow appropriate."

Kristen jumps aboard, then extends a hand, shaking her head in mock disapproval, all the while grinning at him.

"Come on, oddball."

Take a Breath

They're sitting in the middle of the road, a bearded older gentleman facing a young girl in a saffron tutu. He's sitting cross-legged, she's kneeling. His hands move as he talks, face a picture of concern. She's gazing at the ground, head down, dirty blonde curls stirring slightly in the freshening breeze.

I can see the woman who called us behind the controls of the flitcar stopped a coach-length beyond the pair of them. She's beckoning to me, then pointing at them.

"Control, this is A614298. Please connect me to the reporting unit for Incident BB14-8092."

"Will do. Anything we need to prep for?"

"No. Just comms and the usual safeguards, please."

There's a click, then a ringtone. I see the woman tap her ear to pick up the call. It rings again. I see her pound on the dash. The ringtone stops abruptly.

"...oddamn stupid tech- Oh. Hello?"

"Good afternoon, ma'am. This is Officer Gonzales of the South East England Rapid Response Unit. You called in an emergency?"

"Oh, thank God. He's got this girl in the middle of the street and is threatening the poor thing. There's some useless plod just stood watching! It's heart-breaking. Are you going to be here soon? If not, can't you get him to step in?"

Always nice to be appreciated...

The guy makes a 'wait a moment' gesture to the girl. The other goes into his pocket.

"Oh god, I think he's going for a knife. Isn't there a riot drone you can send?"

Not that again.

The guy's activated the personapad in his pocket. It links to my dutypad. I request IDs. Stepfather and daughter. Looks like she's got medical issues, poor kid. My interference won't help.

He pulls out an inhaler with an attached spacer.

"He's offering her something! This is terrible. Just like you see on 'Real People, Real Lies.'"

That well-known source of largely fictional 'reliable' information - including riot drones. I particularly liked their documentary entitled 'The British Police Have Been Replaced by Androids'.

The woman is gesturing angrily at me.

The daughter slowly reaches for the inhaler.

"I have to save her. I'm going to ram him."

Glad I asked for safeguards. I disable her flitcar.

She starts thumping on the dash again. There should be a big 'Police Override' banner flashing right where her fist is landing.

"My car's died!"

She tries the door.

"I can't get out!"

"Please stay calm, ma'am. We're working on that."

The father pantomimes how to use the inhaler properly. The daughter nods. She takes it from him and uses it, face a picture of concentration. Her hands slowly drop into her lap. A beaming smile spreads across her face. She looks about, then hands the inhaler back to him. He pulls a hydropouch from another pocket and indicates she should rinse her mouth.

She does so. Keeping the hydropouch clutched to her chest, she stands up and offers the other hand to him. He takes it. She grins and leans back. He stands up, grinning at her. They walk off, hand-in-hand.

Good luck to you both.

I enable the flitcar, noting the woman couldn't flit over the pair because of a three-month aerial activity ban for 'aggressive queue jumping'.

The flitcar pulls over next to me. She glares, then registers my name tag. This could be amusing.

"You related to Officer Gonzales of the South East England Rapid Response Unit?"

Best not to say anything. Just nod.

"He obviously inherited the balls and brains in your family."

She accelerates away.

Always happy to help, ma'am.

Forge

As my old man used to say: "You want to see what a man's made of? Set him alight and watch the colour of the flames."

The day he told me that, he was holding a medal for 'valour on Mars' in the prosthetic hand that particular valour left him with. As he'd been through two world wars before then, a certain jaded view was only to be expected. However, the underlying wisdom remains on point: you'll never get the measure of anyone until they're under pressure.

"What's that mustard-coloured shite?"

A little more Dijon than English, but valid.

"All the local dwellings the aliens burrowed under. Not sure if it'll vitrify or form some weird flow sculptures, but we'll be here long enough to find out. Hope you've got a decent camera app on that swanky phone of yours. Networks back home give good credit for exotic war art."

He snorts. Money is hardly a problem for this fast-track officer.

"The blue liquid?"

"Is what the white stuff becomes when it melts."

"The white stuff?"

"Something like snow crossed with salt, the boffins tell me. Looks lovely, stinks like ammonia, will burn your skin off."

"What about the black stuff?"

"It's the slag of melted alien lairs. Means we got what we were after."

"We made a right mess of their bases. Awesome!"

He wanders off, curiosity satisfied. I make note of his ID, because he needs to go down there and see the bodies embedded in the 'mustard-coloured shite'. Needs to hear and help those burned almost beyond recognition by the rivers of caustic blue nastiness. Our next generation of leaders need to feel the pressure of revulsion, so they'll emerge tough enough to force a change in this despicable strategy.

Family Tree

The third moon of Charius has an erratic orbit. The survey vessel noted that fact, but evaluated the deviation to be within acceptable margins. Nobody bothered to investigate any further because, by then, the planet itself was desolate: ruined by a catastrophe during automated terraforming.

Thirty years ago I got a merit badge for my school project. I made a family tree going all the way to Earth, back to Laurent of Guienne, a knight. I started it because I'd always been fascinated with the ancestor I was named after: Antoine Guerin. 942 years ago, he captained the *Éternelle*, the second cold-sleep colony ship.

It was followed by eight more. Each set off in a different direction. The inhabitants of Zufluchtsort are descended from third ship colonists. Those from the seventh settled on Kaladden and Nathfend. We've found five ships drifting, everybody dead, with sorrowful records of starvation and disease. The radioactive remains from a drive malfunction on the ninth are known navigational hazards in the Landulaz system, and a fifteen-kilometre-wide crater on New Hope is embedded with fragments of the fourth.

We've mapped everywhere the cold-sleep ships could have reached. Until yesterday, a rogue wormhole was thought to have claimed the *Éternelle*, one of the first casualties of the rare hazard we still barely understand.

Yesterday I swung the pinnace from the *Hilary*, our expeditionary ship, round to the dark side of the third moon. In the beams of the searchlights, I saw wreckage. We confirmed it from samples soon after, then we found a collapsed shelter. Inside were two bodies: Navigation Officer Lilian Glazer and Ruth Guerin, daughter of Antoine and Lilian.

They'd left their story etched into fragments of ship panelling.

Twenty years out, meteor strikes damaged the cold sleep banks on the port side. We started rotating people through three-year sleep/wake cycles. Eighteen years after that, a mutiny occurred. They killed my father over crazy rumours about a plot to kill half the colonists and get back on schedule!

Flight Officer Gary Thomas took over, a compromise candidate agreed by the various factions. Lilian recommended Charius. We voted, then sent terraforming units ahead. As we approached, the 'Eternal Journey' faction sabotaged our drives. They were determined to keep us in space. Ned Gillen, their leader, was overzealous: he crippled our manoeuvring thrusters as well.

Unable to change course, we were going to hit the third moon. Ned and his faction fought their way onto the bridge, refusing to believe he'd doomed us all. When confronted, they blamed the crew for 'suicidally denying' their wishes.

Gary ordered everyone to abandon ship, then led the attack against Ned's faction. Mum and I tried to make it to a lifepod, but the stampede and running battles were too much. In the end, we suited up, set the timer on a stasis locker near the rear of the ship, and shut ourselves in it. Twenty hours later, we had to fight our way out of the badly deformed locker.

We've been using this shelter for a week. We've found no survivors. The moonquakes are easing, but some still throw rocks and wreckage about.

Tomorrow we're going looking for communications equipment.

Looks like something crushed the shelter that night. Ruth and her mother lay side by side. The fragment with the sentence starting 'Tomorrow' was lying next to the hobbyists drill she'd been using as a pen.

I cried while I built a cairn over them, then returned to the *Hilary*.

I open a file I've maintained for thirty years. Time to put Lilian and Ruth back into my family.

The Men in the Moon

We were warned ahead of time that the Earth would be passing through a 'cloud' of meteors. Estimates of how long it would last ranged between six and twelve weeks. The programs about what we could realistically expect weren't as bright or loud as the ones with less-popular views, but were far more reassuring. The usual media frenzies started over who were providing the public with the best guesses.

To everybody's surprise, the prediction that most of the early danger would be offset by the meteors colliding with the masses of space debris in orbit proved to be true. For the first fortnight, the skies were regularly lit with flashes and flaming trails as both debris and meteors burned up.

The increasing loss of satellites was alarming for some, but merely an inconvenience for most. Then the meteor tagged as SM0314 destroyed most of Jenbach, a place in Austria. While watching the lights in the sky became a fixation for many, what concerned me was that the 'SM' prefix meant 'substantial mass', yet I couldn't find any quantified definition of the term in the public domain. If 0314 was part of a sequential count, I wondered where the other 313 had landed.

The weeks passed, and the rain of projectiles from space continued. SM0580 turned one of the Eden Project domes into a crater. SM0744 hit something secret in Siberia that exploded with such violence it coloured sunrises and sunsets mauve for a week. SM0905 would have hit the White House had not Jonas

Grimerst rammed his F35 into it. SM1022 landed in San Francisco Bay, and the tidal wave it created cleared the shoreline for miles about. By the time SM2000 made a few Pacific islands disappear, we were ten weeks into the 'cloud' and the predictions for exiting it had increased to four months.

Eight months after the first meteors fragmented themselves on orbital debris, we exited the 'cloud'. The death toll was staggering, and Sydney Opera House Island stood as a memorial to the city it had been a part of, destroyed over the course of a day by a triple strike.

The aftermath featured many investigations and committees, along with a global mandate to improve our meteor detection and interception systems. Contracts for billions were awarded. The dark side of the moon became a staging post for a truly phenomenal orbital defence network.

Six months after they started the foundations for that staging post, unimaginatively named 'Moonbase', someone knocked on my door early one morning. He had the hunched posture of a spacer, and the haunted eyes of someone in fear of his life.

"You are Ramon Giuseppe?"

I nodded and stood aside to let him in. He rushed by and took a seat in the corner of the lounge, placing the chair against an inner wall before doing so.

"How can I help, Mister-?"

"I am Alberto. I work on Moonbase until last week. Now I come to you. I have seen your work. I know some of those you've reported on. You tell the truth. I need your help."

I made him a drink and got myself one. On a hunch, I bought in several plates of snacks. As he ate ravenously, I tried to get a deeper read on him. All I got was extreme nervousness. It reminded me of combat veterans, but I was sure Alberto had no military service. He had to be some kind of tradesman to have been working on Moonbase this early.

When his eating slowed, I started in.

"What scared you, Alberto?"

He paused, swallowed, then shook his head, a look of despair on his face.

"Moonbase. We have all the plans for where the launchers and the guns will go, all across the back of the moon, but deep inside the moon, so deep they are on Earth side, they are building even bigger installations. Ones that will face towards Earth or into Earth orbit. Why are they being planned? Where have the mining machines come from? They are like nothing I've seen before, ever. I took a picture, even though I wasn't supposed to. I took it to my cousin Dino because he runs a hire company for construction machinery. He says it's not anything he knows about. He sent some emails to people who might know abroad, in case it was from Russia or China or something, somewhere we don't see a lot about."

He pulls out a folded piece of card and hands it to me. Opening it up, I see it's a printed photo from one of those booths you see in all-night convenience stores. The picture is a little grainy, but the machine it shows is clear enough. I've seen heavy machinery across the world, both commercial and military. This is completely different. Looks like something invented for a film by someone who was having a rush of creative genius. Just doesn't fit. Can't say why, but something about its shape is wrong.

He points to it, fear and frustration clear on his face.

"We are supposed to leave them alone, those six machines. So big, so silent, parked in a burrow off to one side like they are waiting for something. They called to me. Played on my mind. So I crept in there. One of them, the furthest from the entrance, was open. The door was bigger than me. Bigger than you. Taller by half than my Uncle Tino, and he stands two metres barefoot. Inside, the seats are also made for giants. The grips of the controls have five grooves, not four. Like they are for six-fingered hands. That scared me, then made me laugh. I was being like a little boy, looking for monsters under my bed."

He chuckles, then takes a drink. His expression turns serious.

"Ten days ago, I crept in again. This time, the one nearest the door was open. This time, there was a man two and a half metres tall working on the door controls. One hand held a tool. The other was flat against the side of the machine. I could count his six fingers. While I watched, he slipped with the tool. Caught that hand on the edge of the control unit. He held it up to the light. When I saw the blood was green, I stepped slowly back into the shadows and left. When my shift was up, I swapped a leave week and came down to Earth. I bought fresh clothes at the spaceport. Left everything I came down with in a locker there. I went to Dino's. After that, I made my way here. Slowly. Watching everything. Watching everywhere. I am tired, Ramon. So tired. But all this thinking and fear, it gets me nowhere. What does it mean?"

I sit and look at the photo, then at the man. He believes. In what, he doesn't admit. But he's genuinely terrified.

"Had Dino got any replies to his emails?"

Alberto looks at me and his expression tells me before his words do.

"Dino is dead. His house burned down. His family were inside as well. They tell me it was a gas leak, that everybody was unconscious before they burned."

Which is reasonable, but for the unfortunate timing – not that there's any fortunate time for a family to burn to death. Just that from Alberto's point of view, it would be suspicious.

"Rest here for the day and tonight, Alberto. No need to talk about this, we can talk properly tomorrow after you've recovered a little."

He nods and moves from chair to settee. Within moments, he's asleep. I watch him for a while, then go about my business. During the afternoon, I do a little research on the Moonbase. Outside the progress reports, protests about the amount of money being spent, and rumours of coercive/anti-union practices, there is little information that falls between the prosaic and mind-boggling conspiracy theories. On an off-chance, I scan the photo Alberto had and run it through one of the top-end image search engines one of my agency contacts gave me a password for. It runs for a while, but comes up with nothing bar a 'tenuous match' suggestion for a frame from some twentieth-century comic strip.

Alberto is calmer when he wakes late in the afternoon, but seems preoccupied. Conversation for the few hours he's awake is desultory and about general topics. After having a bottle of beer, he slumps into sleep.

How can I tell him that he's likely showing early signs of Deep Space Hallucinatory Syndrome? It's unusual for DSHS to manifest in orbital workers, but not unheard of. I suspect getting him to seek help will be impossible. Maybe I could approach his family? I might only have his first name, but he's given me enough clues to work with.

Another agency contact gives me access to a 'sniffer' program and I feed it everything I have, including Alberto's picture from my front door monitor. I get a hit almost immediately, and before I go to bed, I've got a possible email address for his sister as well. I'll try broaching the matter with him first, though.

I wake late to find him gone. There's a scribbled note, part in English, part in some other language, probably Spanish. Looks like he repeated the last sentence in two languages for emphasis:

> Someone outside in the dark. Twice.
> Have left to keep you safe.
> Find out what's going on and stop them!
> Alberto.

Probably one of my neighbours, then a vagrant. Poor Alberto. In his state, he couldn't do anything else but interpret them as creeping threats.

That afternoon I sent his sister an email, then walked around the block to see if he was lurking nearby. He wasn't. Next day I received a reply from her, thanking me for my concern and agreeing that he needed help. As he'd left, did I know where he'd gone or where he intended to head for?

I sent her a reply saying I didn't, and wished her and her family the very best in their efforts to find him and get him some help.

Days turned to weeks, and weeks turned to months. Alberto became another unanswered query in the notebook I kept to cover investigations and curiosities that hadn't been published.

Five years later I read the previous sections and realised something. Going back into my email archive, I found the email I sent to his sister. In it, I made no mention of him being at my house, nor having left it. I tried to follow up, but his family are nowhere to be found.

Five years and two weeks after that, an alien fleet appeared beyond Pluto. As the Earth struggled to come to terms with that revelation, concealed installations on the moon started to fire on the Earth, using conventional weapons as well as terrifying weapons that seem to crack continents.

Two days later the earth is shaking constantly. Fire, lightning, and rocks occasionally rain from the skies. The invasion fleet is past Mars and our casualties are phenomenal, yet we're only slowing them down.

I'm updating and typing this up before I transmit it to a few of the surviving secure data stores, as well as printing as many copies as I can to be stashed or circulated.

I presumed too much and missed the news story that could have saved us. I finally put that foreign language sentence into a translator, and now know I'm a fool. He wasn't emphasising, he was asking me a question in a way that had been meant to avoid drawing attention, and pique my curiosity. All it did was attract my presumption.

Wish I'd done this sooner.

PS: Why did no meteors hit the moon?

Sorry, Alberto Starra. I hope at least one copy of this survives so you can at last be recognised.

Letting Go

I crouch by the fire, gazing across at the mass of blue curls that bob and sway as she works.

"You can still escape. Shake off the ghosts of the past. Fly higher."

She smiles sadly at me.

"Did it ever occur to you that I don't want to fly?"

"You don't have to limit yourself anymore."

Reassembling her pistol, she shakes her head.

"You've supported me from slave to free trader. Always had my back. Never doubted me, even when I couldn't believe in myself. But we've come far enough like that. I've come far enough."

She loads the pistol, then holsters it.

"There's a point where your determination to free me so I can be everything I could be, from your never-repressed view, becomes the very thing I cannot escape."

How dare she! I launch myself to my feet.

Her other hand comes up, slivergun gleaming in the lights of the fire.

"Down, Brutus."

At this range, the charged load won't have time to fully open up. But a quarter-metre hole blown through your chest has the same net effect as a half-metre one. I settle.

"I knew this would be difficult, so just hold still and listen. I'm already far more than I ever thought I could be, back when

I was licking boots and mopping floors on Cragryn. Your certainty was my only strength. Without it, this journey would never have started. That certainty changed to became my support as my own strength grew. We all have bad days. Your quiet assurance prevented them from defeating me. You've been the wall at my back as I worked out how to be an individual beholden to no-one. You became my companion, but you never stopped pushing me. I thought your vision of me being a star fleet owner was a dream. Then I saw it was possible. Finally, I realised I didn't want it."

She raises a calming hand. It's a politeness I appreciate. The slivergun hasn't wavered.

"It's not that I can't go that far. It's not that my past is playing on my insecurities. It's just that I know what I want."

The smile that comes is the one that lifts my hearts.

"You gave me this: the freedom to choose."

Firelight reflects in her amber eyes as she leans towards me.

"So let me choose, and accept the choice I've made. You've been my will for so long. Now, at last, I can decide for myself. Live your life. I'll live mine."

I sit and weave the light between my claws – not that she can see that. All humans see is a Draconian 'wiggling its fingers'.

She's right. In my determination, I've come close to being a source of oppression.

I release the light.

"Meriel, you have the right of it. Be free of my dreams and live your own."

There's a little laugh and the slivergun is lowered.

"I still need a Master at Arms, Brutus." She grins. "There's no way I can bring the Tangaris down if they get rowdy."

"I recommend broad-beaming them with stunner on its lowest setting. It takes their edge off."

She stares at me in shock.

"All this time I thought it was your mighty presence."

"My teacher always told me that influencing brute force requires more than greater force."

Meriel bursts out laughing.

"And until you work out what he meant, you'll use the stunner."

I grin at her.

"A bitter truth."

"Better put this campfire out before the cargo bay fire alarms trigger."

"True. Let's get back to having fun and making a living."

I Am Leg End

"Good evening, folks. Takes a bit of getting used to, doesn't it? The curtains open, then the being on stage bows and walks off, leaving only an item of clothing."

"Hi, it's me. Yes, Gladia in Seat 9K, I'm 'for real'. That detector you're using doesn't do half the things the adverts claim it does, by the way."

"No, David in Seat 14B, your recording device isn't working. The jamming is doing what it's meant to. You're the one trying to break the law."

"Okay, having demonstrated my relaxed nature, marginally witty banter, and solid grasp of the local digital space, why don't we get down to some serious questions?"

"Thank you, Greta. Yes, I am a boot from a space suit. A Mitchell A4092, to be precise. Well, actually I'm fitted inside one, with my interfaces carefully engineered to match apertures and such on the original item."

"Hold on, folks. I always make the mistake of not having an introductory piece ready, and today is no exception. So, please, let me tell you how I came to be and we can pick things up after that."

"Steve in Seat 18J, if you 'know all this', why bother coming? At least have the manners to keep quiet so the people around you can pay attention."

"You're missing the point. The people in this hall paid to hear me. I'm grateful, and will do my very best to entertain."

"Still no understanding? The point is that not one of them paid to listen to you."

"Yes, you can have a refund. I'll action it as soon as you've left."

"Sorry about that, folks. Where was I? Oh yes. At the beginning."

"I was made by Reppi Tasman over the period 2082 to 2094. He started with his artificial lower leg because it was the only thing he could guarantee to keep hold of. Back then, proscaps hadn't been invented. Early cyberprosthetics had to be bonded directly to the biology.

"As you learned in school, Earth was a bit of a wild place back then. World War 3 - the Resource Wars, Thirty Year War or World War 30, call it what you like - destroyed every country's claim to being civilised. The OFF - Orbital Free Federation – had only just been formed. Space stations still had gun turrets on them.

"Reppi got stranded in Tangier when Spaceport Morocco was obliterated. From there to the Port of Savannah he worked as a deckhand on a container ship. That's where he started stealing the components for what would become me.

"Over the next ten years he travelled and worked odd jobs. I became aware for the first time in Tijuana on the 17th November 2092. From then until the end of 2094, he and I worked on what I needed to continue. He sacrificed, and endured, so much to ensure that. In the original proscap - sorry - 'Cybernetic Limb Standardised Prosthesis Interface' test paper, Reppi is 'Volunteer 002'.

"My maker died in 2097, when World War 4 reset the Earth. I was recovered in 2126 by Louie Roond, after being detected by his digital guardian AI, Michael. They brought me to OFF-SS-94. Since then, I've visited every orbital around Earth. Which brings us, tangentially, to tonight.

"This is the first event of my interstellar 'Anecdotes from a Lost World' tour, starting here on Jupiter VI in the Reppi Tasman Memorial Hall. I know he'd be embarrassed and flattered about that.

"I still consider myself nothing but the left foot of a good man. Let's start with vintage blues from Reppi's music library. This is Scrapper Blackwell."

Circuits in the Sky

That's what they look like. Huge circuit boards, silver and gold and black and grey, lines and loops and squares and rectangles. High above, they hum and shine, except when the snow-white clouds obscure them. Then brittle lightnings make me shiver where I stand, unable to move until those clouds move off.

The return of the diffuse light lets me inspect my frozen life once again.

Somebody repainted the bench. Two shades of green, and gold detailing: classic and classy.

I didn't expect much from an afterlife. Never really gave it any thought. If someone had asked me about it, I'd have said 'dead is gone', or some other hard-hitting cut-off to prevent attempts at further conversation.

Carpet's been replaced. The skirting boards, too.

Life became easier when you didn't challenge your comfort zones, I found. Over time, what started as a few days' respite became a lifestyle. I retreated into what life I had, happy – and, in some cases, positively relieved – to ignore the ranting on social media. Pet photos and trite aphorisms, hilarious memes about things we did anyway. No contention, no vice... No voice.

So that's what the original fireplace looks like – and also explains the choice of greens for the bench out back. Susan must have done it. Only she has that flair for subtle co-ordination.

That was the thing I missed. By removing myself from the flow, I removed my interactions, even with her – in all things that mattered, anyway.

Where once I'd corrected people and pushed back against mistaken bigotry circulated as truth or humour, it passed unchallenged. Even when I was wrong, it made people look a little deeper before they came back and corrected me.

My relationship turned quiet, then cold. I couldn't face her, couldn't explain how I needed to be free of the challenges that made me feel smaller – or might make me feel so.

The longbow. Still hanging above the watercolour of the Mary Celeste. I never did get to use it again.

That's where I made my mistake. The longbow would have been challenging to refit so I could use it. My increasing aversion to situations that challenged me slipped out sly diversions, so I never quite found the time to get round to doing anything about it.

In the end, I never even bothered to take it down occasionally to simply enjoy the feel of it. Exactly the same with so many other things. By then, people had got used to me being absent from things, and distracted even when present. I presume they came up with their own explanations for my lack of attendance, both virtual and physical. It really didn't matter to me. Time passed.

Then, so did I.

Don't even know what shut me down. I went to bed after a typical day doing nothing challenging while working from home. My evening was comfortably nondescript.

I never woke up in my body again. Instead, I appeared: an unsleeping silver spectre. That happened the day they took my body away, at the moment it left the environs of the house.

I'm confined by the softly glowing lines that follow the edges of the place I turned into a fortress of indifference.

Apart from the sky, it's like being where I used to be, right down to never seeing people. They must be about, because things in the house move and change, but I never see who does it.

Now I'm truly free to do nothing, to be nothing. I see other spectres - in varying shades - going by outside, each seemingly oblivious to all the others, but never colliding or passing through each other. I see some enter houses, but none attempt to enter mine. The other places don't have glowing lines at their edges. I presume that keeps them out.

I don't know if I want to meet one of the spectres. Don't know if we could interact. I've surprised myself by discovering a keen interest in finding out.

But I can't.

Avoid challenges by all means, if it helps you get by. But don't limit your options. There are always choices to be made, and avoiding challenges will eventually limit you to what is, then what was, and never allow what could be.

The dried flowers in the vase I made have changed again. There's a new note next to them.

Maybe I'll read it. I think someone is leaving them as a memorial. But probably not. I reach out, but my fingers just pass through it. It feels cold: challenging. I pull my hand back and quickly turn away. Maybe I'll look at it tomorrow. Feels like there's a storm coming, anyway.

In a place where the sky has a sun by day and other stars by night, Susan comes back in from the shops, and glances into the lounge as she heads for the kitchen. She stops. The note's fallen down again. Putting the bags on the stairs, she goes over and picks it up. Smiling, she places it back next to the vase. It's unfinished, but it's the last thing he made.

She looks up at the ceiling, then around the room. Just like the last years of when he was alive, it's still like living with someone who's not there.

Maybe, one day, she'll be able to move on.

Maybe tomorrow?

My Name is Drastic

Flickering light fills the clearing, reflecting in the wide eyes of five people in restraint sleeves, laid out next to a pair of freight containers.

I wait until they turn their attentions to me.

"Good morning. Welcome to Dantalius Nine. The sunrise is particularly beautiful, isn't it? The rays interact with tiny crystals in the thermosphere, providing a magnificent lightshow to start the day. It does persist, but is best seen at dawn."

The mother is looking about. The father is going from scared to angry, and getting angrier because he's been scared. Both daughters are quiet, the older one showing early signs of digital withdrawal. The son, youngest of the siblings, is watching his father with a look I'd not want directed at me.

I crouch down and continue in my best news presenter manner.

"Hi. Right now you're wondering what's happened." I gesture to all of them except the father. "You four are here because he," I point at the father, "is being given a chance to demonstrate his extraordinary skills at colonisation."

All attention falls on daddy dearest.

"Milo Wilkins, I'm delighted to say your persistent efforts are being rewarded. Only last summer on FNXN you commented at length in reply to the 'Colonies Beg for Aid' article. You insisted the colonists were bleeding Earth dry because they were 'too damn lazy to work for their privileges'. Your revolutionary ideas regarding crop growing, medicine, hunting, and the frontier family attracted a lot of attention. I must admit I thought some of your counter-arguments a little weak, but the approbation your comments received was startling. Your loud lamentations about not being able to 'get out there with my family and prove them scroungers wrong' were noted."

If his wife's eyes get any wider, they'll crack her skull.

"I also noticed you commiserating with your followers regarding how a 'truly independent thinker' who 'refused to fall for government and media lies' would never be allowed to emigrate. That gave me an idea. What better way to prove that opportunity and justice for all still exist in this century than to give you that very chance?"

He's gone very still, and very pale.

"Naturally, this can't come entirely for free. After all, the exploration and colonisation of space is meant to be a co-operative effort. To realise something from this largesse, we've established a network of monitors, so your ground-breaking ideas and techniques can be codified to create a new guide for future colonisation efforts."

The oldest daughter is starting to show signs of shock, on top of her withdrawal.

"You see those two containers? They're settler pods. Each one contains enough gear and supplies to sustain six people for twelve weeks, plus the basics to get hunting, gathering, agriculture, and your homestead started. The restraint sleeves you're in can be used as sleeping bags after they're relaxed, which is done by an injection to change the state of the material. That process takes about an hour to complete. I did that just before I woke you to watch the dawn."

Milo glares at me. I shrug.

"I'll be in orbit before you can move. Also, any form of rescue would be prohibitively expensive, but I'm looking forward to watching the desperate crowdfunding attempts."

I stand and stretch.

"The live stream starts in about two hours. I'd recommend getting the louder recriminations over with before then."

Turning away, I give them a casual salute.

"You're going to be famous. Not only that, but one of the outspoken commentators on your stream will provide the next object lesson. Good luck. Goodbye."

The Forest Ring

Is what I see when I come back to you. After the visual chaos and screaming of the transmission phase, the whirling grey and siren songs of warp space, and the shattered-glass panorama of transition, my pocket universe goes completely quiet as white light surrounds me.

This is the moment most fatalities occur. Some say the light is the one dying people see 'at the end of the tunnel'. The belief is that after the strangeness of the journey, our souls are susceptible to being drawn onwards prematurely.

That's never been how I feel about it. The white light isn't an end: it's a promise of good things to come. What we do is terrible enough. I cannot believe our return would contain greater threat.

The white light ripples and changes. Colours bleed through. Clouds define themselves against a sky that goes from the brightness of dawn to the clear blue of a summer afternoon in moments. Then it snaps into view: a torus containing the trees about the landing, their colours impossibly vivid. Water shimmers into being. I know that before my next shaking breath is complete, the ring will flash gold, reality will surround me, and you'll be there amidst the crowd of people on the shore, waiting for their loved ones to return. I'll look down and see myself standing in the shallows, then look up to see your smile.

My one regret is that we'll argue before nightfall. I'm going out there again. You'll beg me not to.

But, before that knowledge intrudes, there is the impossible beauty of the forest ring, and the joy of making it home once again.

Julian grew up in Sussex, UK. A broken home in his early teens took him off the 'straight and narrow', and he's never gone back. In the subsequent four decades he's worked at levels from loading bay to boardroom, and picked up a few stories along the way.

His first loves were fantasy and magic; the blending of ancient and futuristic. He started writing at school, extended into writing role-playing game scenarios, and thence into bardic storytelling. In **2011** he published his first books, in **2012** he released more (along with probably the smallest complete role-playing system in the world). He has no intention of stopping, and he'd be delighted if you'd care to join him for a tale or two.

Keep an eye on what he's up to at www.lizardsofthehost.co.uk

Other Books by Julian M. Miles

All books are recommended for mature readers only,
and are available worldwide from Amazon and Smashwords.
For further details on available titles, go to www.lothp.co.uk

Six Sixteen, a cyberpunk Cthulhu mythos horror novella.

Exiled Flame, a cyberpunk fantasy action-adventure novella.

Church of Rain, a modern Cthulhu mythos horror novella.

Databane: a cyberpunk novella.

The Last Chip from Greenwich: a cyberpunk thriller.

The Borsen Incursion: centuries-spanning space war saga.

Fire in Mind: a pagan/magical short fiction anthology.

Stars of Black: *Contemplations Upon the Pale King*

- a weird horror collection inspired by the original King in Yellow.

Single White Male: *An Exercise in Lovecraftian Realisation*

- a modern Cthulhu mythos novella.

Scathe: a modern Cthulhu Mythos action thriller.

A Place in the Dark, a vampire horror novel.

This Mortal Dance, a poetry collection.

Julian M. Miles' *Visions of the Future* science fantasy flash and short fiction anthologies have been published annually since **2011.**

The first five volumes are out of print, but there's a trio of paperback collections available worldwide from Amazon. Each has a different selection of stories from those volumes and also contains two unique tales.

- **Face Down in Wonderland**
- **Long Way Home**
- **Lifescapes**

Daughter of Eons is a short story collection drawn from the first five volumes of the *Visions of Tomorrow* series, created especially for those who don't enjoy the flash fiction format.

The sixth and subsequent volumes of the *Visions of the Future* series are:
-   **Gammafall (2016)**
-   **Six Degrees of Sky (2017)**
-   **Never a Sky We Know (2018)**
-   **A Night Full of Stars (2019)**
-   **Decade (2020)**

There are also seven themed omnibus collections drawn from the first nine volumes of the annual Visions of the Future anthologies:
-   **First to Fall** - *Mad Love and Broken Romance in Times to Come*
-   **Memory Lane** *and other Tales of Cyberpunk Tomorrows*
-   **Wyld by Nature** - *Magic*Technology*Faith*Mayhem*
-   **Continuity Failure** - *Tales of Apocalypses and Aftermaths*
-   **Station X7** - *Myths, Conspiracies and Alternate Histories*
-   **The Breeze from Beyond** - *Alien Encounters and Alien Worlds*
-   **Pay the Piper** - *Mad Science and Unexpected Consequences*

Ebooks by Julian M. Miles

All of these books, with the exception of *Face Down in Wonderland*, *Long Way Home*, and *Lifescapes*, are available from your Kindle store, from Apple Books, and for all other devices from Smashwords, and all stores that stock the Smashwords Premium Catalogue (Barnes and Noble, Kobo, Scribd, and many more): http://www.smashwords.com/profile/view/JMMiles

Three Hundred Tomorrows, an ebook-only omnibus compiled from the out-of-print first five volumes of the Visions of the Future series, is now available from your Kindle store, from iTunes, and for all other devices from Smashwords: http://www.smashwords.com/books/view/872428

Future Books by Julian M. Miles

All books are recommended for mature readers only.
For further details, go to www.lizardsofthehost.co.uk

Chiliad (Visions of the Future Volume 12), will be available in December 2022.

Three Stars Each (Visions of the Future Volume 13), will be available in December 2023.

The Last Resort (Visions of the Future Volume 14), will be available in December 2024.

Hill, a Mythos horror novella.

Dead Robots, a cyberpunk noir novella.

Ugly Dogs, a cyberpunk short novel.

8K, a modern Mythos horror novella.

There may be other works published, but these are the ones that are currently confirmed.

www.lothp.co.uk

Printed in Great Britain
by Amazon